GETTING OVER HARRY

GETTING OVER HARRY

BY
RENEE ROSZEL

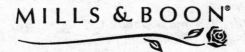

MILLS & BOON®

To my son, Randy, with love

First published in Great Britain 1996
Large Print edition 1997
Harlequin Mills & Boon Limited,
Eton House, 18-24 Paradise Road,
Richmond, Surrey TW9 1SR

© Renee Roszel Wilson 1996

ISBN 0 263 14920 X

Set in Times Roman 16 on 17½ pt.
16-9701-53913 C

Printed and bound in Great Britain
by Mackays of Chatham PLC, Chatham, Kent

CHAPTER ONE

EMILY couldn't believe she was a guest in a magnificent mansion, and that she was such a *liar*. Well, maybe she wasn't a liar yet. But any minute now—when the mysterious owner of Sin Island showed himself—she would *become* a liar. It was true, she'd wanted to make changes in her life, but turning into an unscrupulous fake hadn't been one of them.

She veered off her usual jogging route along the manicured lawn and headed for a white sand beach, luminescent and vaguely pink in the pale dawn. The only sound besides the dull thud of her shoes was the lapping of the surf. Wasn't that low roar supposed to be calming? She hoped so. She needed the serene rush of the waves to help ease her frazzled emotions.

She quickened her pace as she raced through the damp sand. Her lungs were burning, but she had to block out the guilt. What better way than with physical torture? And jogging certainly *was*. She was in agony.

Maybe she'd be lucky and die of a heart attack before she had to go through with the awful sham.

She raced along at breakneck speed, her heart pounding so hard she feared it would explode. To ease her burning lungs, she gulped pungent, salt-laden sea air. It didn't help. When the beach ended, she sprinted up an incline, rounding a barrier of palms, ferns and cypress trees.

Pain exploded in her shin and she cried out as she lost her footing, rolling once, possibly twice. She was so disoriented she couldn't be sure. When she came to rest a little way down a grassy slope, she was breathing hard and smarting in a number of places. Her shin stung, her hip burned and her shoulder throbbed.

Shaky, she pushed up on one elbow, rubbing her shoulder. What in heaven's name had she stumbled over? Maybe one of the rules of jogging was to check the route for cliffs and chasms before running blindly along. She groaned, touching her shin where a bruise was blossoming.

"Are you all right?"

She heard the masculine voice at the same instant she felt someone grasp her upper arm. "Can you stand?"

Befuddled and breathless, she was slow to respond, or even to be sure she wasn't hallucinating.

"Miss?" came the deep voice again. "Can you hear me?"

When she managed to lift her gaze in the direction of the query, she froze at the most thrilling sight she'd ever seen. A man loomed before her. His face was very close, for he was crouching beside her. Long, tan fingers gently circled her arm, and his jet black eyes were narrowed with concern. She stared into those eyes. They were absolutely striking, with lashes long enough to shade small mammals.

And those lips! Just full enough to be completely male, they seemed to be fashioned exclusively for kissing. Her heart did an odd flip-flop. What a peculiar thought for a sensible biology teacher to have about an entirely common bit of anatomy.

Though drawn down in concern, the stranger's lips were exactly like those she'd seen on one memorable television commercial selling

shaving cream. Only a square jaw and delicious male lips had been visible. Emily had
a feeling that, as the TV man with the sexy
mouth shaved and shaved, women were
grabbing up their purses, rushing out to buy
shaving cream. She had to admit that even
she had bought that brand for her invalid father a time or two. *Lips*! What a silly explanation for buying a product. But for some
reason—

"Miss?" he asked again, tearing her from
her fanciful stupor. "Can you understand
me?"

She managed a nod, feeling herself color
with embarrassment. From her lack of response he must think she'd received a head
injury. How could she have drifted off like
that? "Of—of course," she whispered
hoarsely. "I'm fine."

His handsome features eased. "Do you
think you can stand?"

She made a mental survey of her aches and
pains and decided she was only bruised, not
broken. With another small nod, she began
to push herself up, but found most of her
upward movement due to his assistance.

She heard a resonant chuckle near her ear. "I've had women fall head over heels for me, but not quite so literally."

Out of the corner of her eye, she saw something. A gray metal box sat in the middle of the path. For the first time, she noticed she was standing in a sheltered cove, hidden from the beach by lush, tropical vegetation. So that's what happened. She'd come around a blind curve and somersaulted over this workman's toolbox.

She felt like a fool for being so clumsy, but for some reason his egotistical remark was more disturbing than her tumble down the hill. With a surge of defensiveness, she mumbled, "If you have to *trip* women to get them to fall for you, it's not much of a victory."

It was only then that she realized he'd straightened to his full height. He was quite tall. Well over six feet. Her gaze skittered to his face, where inky tendrils of hair fell across a broad forehead. Capricious, early morning sunlight took that instant to pay homage to the stranger, highlighting him in a golden aura. The sight was so dazzling, so ethereal, her breath caught. His chest was bare, sinewy and silky with dark hair. He was wearing cutoff jeans that molded taut hips. A tool belt rode his trim waist.

Shifting his weight, he hooked a thumb in his work belt. The ripple of bronzed shoulder muscle caught her attention. She swallowed, staring openly. Those shoulders were a yard wide if they were an inch and held the carved perfection of a Greek statue.

"I'm sorry about my toolbox," he said, a little belatedly for Emily's taste. "Not many people wander onto this side of the island."

His impertinent remark about women falling head over heels for him still nagged at her, making her peculiarly defiant. "So—so you felt free to barricade the path?" Something inside her was very disappointed that this man was so much less a gentleman than he was handsome. She supposed he was terribly spoiled by women and could get away with anything where they were concerned. Well, not around *her*, he couldn't!

"I didn't mean to block your path." He settled a boot on a nearby rock. "Actually, I was about to tie my shoe." Her gaze trailed down his long, tanned leg to his booted foot. Sure enough, the laces were loose. "I should be shot for being so thoughtless."

She stiffened at his teasing tone. "Maybe you should," she muttered, fully aware that he was admonishing her for flying off the handle prematurely. Unfortunately, she knew he was right, but she couldn't bring herself to admit it. To avoid his amused glance, she looked away. Something caught her eye.

Perched high above the dawn-washed water of the cove, among luxuriant foliage of wax myrtles, palms and brilliant wild flowers, stood the wooden frame of a cottage under construction. Part of the structure extended out over a rocky bluff toward the sea. Open on three sides, it was brilliantly situated to welcome balmy sea breezes.

It was beautiful in its simplicity, and Emily fell immediately in love with it—wishing it was finished, wishing she could spend her time here on the island in this charming retreat. She knew her heart would mend more quickly in such a peaceful, secluded haven as this. She pulled her lips together, refusing to cry. *Not anymore.*

"I accept your apology," he murmured, bending to tie the laces.

Her gaze snapped to the carpenter, obviously out here to work on this retreat for his aloof, camera-shy boss. As she watched him tie his boot laces, she could only stand there chewing her lower lip. They both knew she hadn't apologized, and they both knew she should, but she couldn't seem to speak.

She could only stare, pondering what a marvelous piece of machinery the human body was—every sleek, supple element working in lithe and limber concert with the others. It was remarkable how much rippling of muscle was involved in the small act of tying a shoe. She found herself intrigued by each bulge and twitch of his arms and shoulders.

"I always thought of jogging as a substitute for sex," he commented as he straightened.

Torn from her trance, she frowned, unsure she'd heard right. *Did the man have the audacity to suggest he kept in such fantastic shape by having sex?* "What—what did you say?"

He grinned. "I said, I always thought of jogging as—"

"Never mind!" she cut in, determined not to give him the chance to say it again. Maybe risqué comments served him well with most women, but the taunt only rankled her already stressed-out nerves. "For your information, I've heard the same thing about *hammering*!" She was shocked at herself. Where had *that* come from? She supposed she'd seen the hammer hanging from one of the loops in his belt, and some defensive instinct deep inside her demanded to be heard. Mortified, she faced the fact that she really did need to apologize now.

A rumble of laughter split the tense quiet. The sound tingled along her spine, heating her skin. She'd planned to turn on her heel and make a quick escape—after her apology— but the deep-throated chuckle held her like the cascading waterfall from a healing hot spring.

Laugh lines appeared at the corners of his eyes, and long, cleaving dimples creased his lean cheeks. Again she was reminded of the shaving cream commercial. She had an urge to ask him if he'd ever been on TV, but decided that would only swell his already billowing ego.

"You have a surprising wit," he said, still chuckling.

She bristled, her apology dying on her lips. "Well, you're *conceited*, and I'm not at all surprised."

His smile never wavered. "Are you saying I deserve to be?"

He was certainly smooth, standing there laughing at her, turning her insult into a compliment. She wanted to slap his face and stalk off, but an idea pestered her and she couldn't quite get it to die.

This guy was cocky and smug, but she couldn't deny he exuded a rugged sexuality and was clearly a rogue where women were concerned. Even though the idea of giving him another ego boost appealed to her about as much as being struck by lightning she was in dire need of the knowledge he possessed— practically flaunted!

Besides, no matter how badly it had begun, she *had* struck up a conversation with him. And he *had* called her witty. Maybe he wasn't completely disinterested in her. Unconsciously, she tugged on her jogging shorts, unaccustomed to showing off so much leg— especially to a man who was plainly an expert on the subject of women's legs. She swallowed with difficulty, wondering if she had the nerve to do what her best friend, Meg, had been nagging her to do.

Her heart was pounding so furiously she was afraid she would have a heart attack, after all, but not from jogging—from pure cowardice. This was the nineties, for heaven's sake. Women took the initiative all the time these days. They *asked* for what they wanted.

Could fate have stepped in—in the form of a badly placed toolbox—giving her this chance? If she was ever going to learn what she needed to know, would this be her only opportunity? Could she let fate down? Could she let herself down? Did she *dare* let Meg down?

Evidently some of her best friend's uninvited counsel had started to sink in, for here she was, rooted to the ground beside this overbearing, self-serving egotist, actually thinking the unthinkable!

She shuddered, vacillating. All she could actually manage at the moment was to delay her huffy departure. Maybe she could work up her nerve. Sucking in a breath, she decided to stall by making conversation. "What— what were we talking about?" she asked faintly.

His gaze was inquisitive, as though he'd been trying to read her thoughts. "I believe you were calling me conceited."

Her glance plummeted to her jogging shoes. "Oh—right..." Her nerve drained away and she began to turn to go. "Well—goodbye."

"Just a second," he said, effectively halting her. "Really. Why the kamikaze jogging?"

She lifted her gaze to his face, a formidable effort. His lips twitched in an inquiring grin that was exasperating and riveting at the same time. Her brain warned, *Emily, it's now or never.* She ran a hand through her straight hair, wanting to scream with frustration. But if she wanted to learn what attracted men, Mr. Conceited Carpenter here seemed to be her best chance. Maybe her only chance. All she needed was the courage to take it.

She forced a smile. "Actually, it's quite simple. I'm jogging to improve myself." Her words were strained, but she doubted that he could tell, since he hardly knew her. Widening her smile and hoping her face wouldn't crack with the effort, she turned in a circle, an experimental effort at flirtation. "I've been running for nearly a week. What—what do you think?"

One dark brow lifted skeptically. "It would be hard to tell much after only a few days."

Though he chose to give her a straight answer to her surface question, she was dismayed by his rebuff to her flirting.

"Exercise is one thing, but don't you think such a breakneck pace is dangerous? Maybe you should walk first."

That did it! Not only was he rejecting her, he was lecturing her as though he was her big brother. Offended, she admonished, "I think you need to learn to mind your own business."

He gave her a look that suggested she wasn't being rational. After all, she'd *asked* his opinion. Embarrassed, she spun around. "Thanks for the physical fitness tip. Feel free to send me a bill.'' She limped away from him, but Meg's disapproving expression wavered before her with every step she took. *You're backsliding, Emily. Don't give up on the first try! Men don't.*

She'd gotten ten feet away when she found herself coming to a halt. Nausea rose in her throat. She'd been a teacher for four years, and she'd been raised by teachers—pragmatic, straightforward people. She wasn't good at subtlety or playfulness, so she was at a loss about how to convince him to do this thing.

Since he'd made it clear she was a failure at flirtation, then what about honesty? Being brutally honest worked for her when she had to remind students that they would fail without studying. But would it work here? She lifted her chin, renewing her determination.

This time, when she met his gaze, she didn't smile, didn't make the slightest effort to flirt. He was quietly watching her. His expression, too, had gone serious. Did he sense her turmoil? She prayed he didn't.

"Say..." she called, trying to sound careless. When the word came out quivery, she cleared her throat.

He didn't respond, but cocked his head to indicate he was listening.

She limped a step in his direction, then stopped. It was humiliating that she even had to ask this. She certainly didn't want to be close to him when he doubled over laughing. "I—I was just wondering. Would you—do you think you and I might..." Her cheeks were fiery, but she hurried to get it said before she lost her nerve for good. "I was wondering if you'd mind, uh, having *sex* with me?" The dreaded word came out in a high-pitched squeak, and she flinched. So much for appearing careless.

His eyes widened for a split second. Or was that her imagination? She couldn't be sure, for she'd stopped breathing some time ago, and she was getting dizzy.

He stared at her for what seemed like a year, his features telling her nothing. Her chest began to ache so badly she no longer noticed the physical injuries she'd sustained. While she waited for his response, she couldn't decide what she wanted his answer to be. If it was no, she'd be demoralized, of course. But if it was yes? My lord! What if it was yes! Could she go through something so intimate with a stranger?

A taunting smile tipped the corners of his lips. ''You mean you want me to have sex with you until you recuperate enough to jog again?''

His eyes had become earthy, twinkling pools of mirth. And there was something else there, too. Was it pity? Had he read the fear in her expression and decided to be compassionate, pretending he thought she was joking? Or had the idea of making love to her been so disgusting he'd reacted in his usual, sarcastic way?

She gritted her teeth. Of course she wasn't naive enough to believe she'd seen compassion in his eyes. That was an insane thought brought on by lack of oxygen. Though she knew she should have been relieved, the rejection was painful. She'd just laid herself wide open before a man who probably thought nothing of a sexual tumble in the grass. And he'd repaid her by teasing her. Blood pounded in her temples, and she knew she must be crimson with shame and fury.

If the truth was told, she was more angry with herself than with him. She shouldn't allow his snub to upset her. She didn't even know this man. So why did she feel almost as deflated by his rejection as she'd felt by her fiancé's public abandonment at the church? How nuts!

The whole idea had been foolish to begin with. Why had she listened to Meg? Evidently her emotional state over Harry's betrayal had driven her a bit mad.

Summoning every ounce of pride to her aid, she glared at him. "Look, buster, don't make the mistake of thinking I'm attracted to you." She shook a finger in his direction. She knew it was exactly the old-fashioned, school-marmish sort of thing she'd decided she must change about herself, but she was too mortified to care. "For one crazy minute, I thought I might try to learn how to become more exciting to men. And, since you're *moderately* good-looking, I felt you might be able to show me a thing or two. Lucky for me, I've come to my senses. The idea was dumb, and if you want my honest opinion, you're the last man on earth I'd—I'd..." For some reason she couldn't say the explicit word again. She was too embarrassed.

"You'd what?" he coaxed.

She sensed compassion in his voice, and that knowledge hurt her worse than his rejection. She was sick and tired of sympathetic looks and whispers and couldn't stand them from this arrogant stranger, too! "Don't you dare pity me!" she cried, tromping off, cringing at the ache in her shin, but forcing herself not to limp.

"What makes you think you need to change?"

"Forget it!" She didn't stop or turn back.

"Look, sweetheart," he called across the growing distance, "there are those who'd say having sex with somebody you don't know won't make you more exciting—just cheap."

She lurched to a halt at his blunt observation. He had a point. But she doubted he attributed that same philosophy to himself. She glared at him over her shoulder. "So, sex between strangers makes a woman *cheap*, but it makes a man a *stud*, right?''

When he pursed his lips but made no response, she continued, ''That's what I thought you'd say.'' Needing to strike back for the humiliation he'd caused, she bluffed, ''I should thank you. You've helped me make a decision. I've decided to have an affair with the owner of this island.'' She was flagrantly lying now, but what difference did it make? This irritating workman would never know the truth. ''I can get *expert* experience at being wild and uninhibited from Lyon Gallant. I've heard he can be very accommodating that way.''

The crooked grin returned to the carpenter's face, causing an odd sizzle in the pit of her stomach. That smile held a cryptic ingredient she couldn't fathom, but she decided it was probably for the best. The man had smut for a mind.

He hooked his thumbs in his work belt with an accompanying ripple of tanned muscle. ''Let me know how the seduction goes.''

''Naturally!'' she shouted. ''Why don't you hold your breath until I come back with the news?'' As quickly as her bruised body would allow, she hurried away, vowing to jog anywhere and everywhere on Sin Island, as long as it was nowhere near this cove—and one particularly rude, offensive hired hand.

After Emily showered and changed into a pair of slacks and a white cotton blouse, she headed downstairs, trying to block Mr. Jogging Is a Substitute for Sex from her mind. As was her habit, she joined Meg and her aunt Ivy in the housekeeper's neat first-floor office, filled with sunlight and the most exquisite antiques Emily had ever seen.

''Morning, Em,'' Meg chirped, as she perched unceremoniously on the edge of her aunt's Queen Anne desk. She looked leggy and lovely in a short red skirt, cropped knit blouse and sandals. ''How was the jog?''

Emily cringed inwardly. ''Fine.'' She decided the less said about her failed attempt at seducing handsome workmen, the better. ''What's on the agenda for today? Do we lie yet?''

Meg's chuckle was always surprisingly big, since she was such a petite woman. Both she and her aunt were tiny, and at five feet six, Emily felt like a lumbering dinosaur next to them. ''Aunt Ivy was telling me our phantom host left a few minutes ago in his helicopter to spend the day in his Miami high-rise. So I guess we're off the hook again.'' Emily heard the wistfulness in Meg's voice. Poor thing couldn't hide her disappointment at *not* getting to see Lyon Gallant, even after being on his island for five whole days.

Ivy Dellin looked up from her datebook. A woman in her early fifties, she had the same intelligent black eyes and hair as her niece, but she wore her tresses in a short, no-nonsense bob. There wasn't a trace of gray in her shiny cap of hair, and Emily knew it was natural. Having gotten to know Ivy over the past week, she'd discovered the woman put on absolutely no airs. She never wore makeup. Even without it, she was striking, and every bit as sweet-natured as she was lovely. Emily had to give Mr. Gallant credit. He knew quality when he saw it.

The major difference between the aunt and the niece was Meg's incessant curiosity. Emily found that inquisitive trait in her friend endearing most of the time. But there were moments lately when her nosiness was downright shameful. She'd given her aunt the third degree over and over this week about what Mr. Gallant looked like. Though he was rumored to be a handsome, sexy scoundrel, the man didn't have a single picture of himself in the house.

Meg's commando tactics on her aunt had done no good. Ivy always remained composed, explaining, "Mr. Gallant values his privacy, Meg, dear. If he wants you to know about him, he'll tell you himself."

"Has he asked about us?" Meg asked for the thousandth time. "Has he noticed us at *all*?"

"He's asked nothing. And he knows just what I told you I'd tell him—that because of a computer malfunction at the interior design offices, there are two decorators here recalculating measurements for the remodeling of the west wing."

"Won't he get suspicious when all the curtains and carpets and wallpaper and stuff come right on schedule?" Meg prodded. "I mean, since there really wasn't a computer foul-up?''

Ivy shrugged, but on her the move was elegant. ''He's too busy to concern himself with household details. He'll merely assume they put a rush on the orders because of the inconvenience.''

Meg nodded, seemingly satisfied. ''And he doesn't even think our being here this long seems—seems unusual?''

''I told Mr. Gallant I'm also consulting the two interior decorators about redoing my quarters and his suite, since that awful movie star, Mona Sabrina, covered herself with paint and rolled her body along his bedroom wall.'' The woman's sweet, ever-poised face screwed up in a grimace. ''The hussy should be spanked.''

Meg's laugh rumbled. ''I'm sure Lyon handled that.''

Ivy's arched brows arched further. ''What?''

''I mean—if she *wanted* him to spank her,'' Meg amended, patting her aunt's lacy shoulder. ''Honestly, Aunt Ivy. You must open your eyes to the real world.''

Ivy stood up and brushed away imaginary wrinkles from her linen skirt. "Mr. Gallant's personal affairs are none of my business—or yours, dear. All I know is, he said he didn't care for Miss Sabrina's body autograph on his bedroom wall, and if my two interior decorators had the extra time, he'd like them to see to the renovation. But you two needn't worry, I've already handled that by phone, and am in the process of picking out fabrics and wallpapers for my quarters from books Demetrius left for me. I can arrange it all by phone."

"Oh! Let me see his room!" Meg begged, taking Ivy's perfectly manicured fingers and bouncing up and down. "Please, oh please! I must see his bedroom!"

Ivy shook her head at her niece. "I'm afraid not. Besides, there aren't any pictures of him in there, if that's your ploy."

Meg flipped her long, thick braid over her shoulder in a fit of pique. "Phooey! Between your loyalty to your boss and his fanatical need for privacy, I'm going to get an ulcer from curiosity."

"That is, of course, your problem, dear," Ivy chided with a smile. "Now, since Mr.

Gallant will be away today, why don't you girls go have a leisurely breakfast?'' She patted Emily's hand. "Then relax by the pool. Emily needs to get her emotional strength back.'' She gave her niece a stern but maternal look. "And you, young lady, need to remember the whole reason you came here was to help perk up Emily's spirits, not invade Mr. Gallant's privacy. In addition, Meg Dellin *Dillburg*, Larry would be appalled to know, while he's away on an archeological dig in Brazil, his wife is consumed with curiosity about another man."

"Oh, Larry's in his element when he's digging up old bones. I'm just showing a little clinical interest in some newer ones, that's all,'' Meg objected with a pout. "My Larry is completely secure in our love. He knows I'm only interested in seeing the guy, not having his babies."

"And perhaps you shall—see him, that is. If he chooses.'' She placed an arm about her niece's shoulders. "You're a nosy miss, but you're my dear, departed sister's little girl, and I love you."

Meg hugged her aunt's waist. "And you're a lovable—if tight-lipped—conspirator, letting us hide out here for awhile. I sure hope you don't get into trouble."

"You know I've never been able to say no to you, Meg." She smiled lovingly at her niece.

Emily knew Meg was all the family Ivy had in the world, and that she would do anything her effervescent niece asked of her. She only hoped this obvious breach in Ivy's strict moral code wouldn't put her in hot water with her boss. Feeling a surge of guilt, she squeezed the older woman's fingers. "If you get fired on my account, I'll never forgive myself."

"Don't fret, dear." Ivy smiled at Emily. "Mr. Gallant spends very little time drawing and quartering his employees, and he never interferes with my operation of the household. Besides, he's hardly ever here."

Meg moaned. "You sure know how to ruin a girl's day."

The older woman's low-pitched titter was contagious, and even in her dour mood, Emily joined in.

The three women walked arm in arm down the long marble hallway toward the kitchen.

"Okay, Aunt Ivy, just tell me this." Meg had taken on her all too familiar inquisition tone. "Is he blond or brunet?"

"I repeat, dear, you're a nosy miss." Ivy shook her head at her niece. "Why can't you be like Emily?" She felt the older woman's affectionate squeeze on her waist. "The dear child hasn't asked one single question about Mr. Gallant."

Emily tried to smile at Meg's aunt, but she felt like a hypocrite. The straitlaced housekeeper would be horrified to discover her outrageous vow to the carpenter in the cove— *about seducing his boss*. She regretted blurting that out, and breathed a silent prayer that she would *never* lay eyes on the elusive Lyon Gallant.

CHAPTER TWO

AFTER her shower, Emily felt unaccountably restless. There were still two hours before dinner, but Ivy simply wouldn't hear of letting her help in the kitchen. She ran a comb through her damp hair, absently staring into the vanity mirror. The guest room she'd been assigned was reflected in the glass. She scanned what she could see of the room. Its colors were light, and a wall of windows made the place seem too airy to be indoors. Yet the eighteenth-century antiques gave the bedroom a solid, courtly feel. She shook her head in wonder, then caught the movement and glanced up to stare into wide, sapphire eyes.

She focused on her face. The sun had put a blush on her cheeks, even through her sun-block, and left a trail of burnished freckles across her nose. She wished bringing out any latent desirability in her was as easy as freckling. She'd be a regular femme fatale by now.

Though she was trying hard to keep her
spirits light and block the dismal memory
from her mind, the letter Harry had left her
on their wedding day came vividly back. She'd
read it in disbelief so many times, she'd com-
mitted it to memory whether she wanted to or
not. "Emily, I'm sorry. I know you'll be hurt,
but I must follow my feelings. Your sister,
Elsa, is so much like you in many ways, only
she's more exciting, what everyvman wants."

Emily's best friend, Meg, had been a loyal
shoulder to cry on after Harry's abandonment, but Emily had paid the price for
Meg's comfort by being force-fed her counsel.
"Sweetie," she'd advised, "men are painfully
simple creatures. Show 'em you have a great
mind *after* you catch their attention with a
well-toned butt and a naughty wiggle."

Emily knew Meg had a point, however
crudely put. Jogging had been her first tentative step at improving herself, though she
was naturally slender. And she'd decided it
wouldn't kill her to mix with new people,
maybe even learn a point or two about
seductiveness. She'd been shamed by the
whispers she'd had to endure in her home-

town—"Poor Emily Stone, the spinster schoolteacher who couldn't hold on to the only man she'd ever caught."

That was why she'd jumped at the chance to leave for awhile. That was also why she hadn't asked Meg many questions about where they were going when her friend suggested this trip—not *enough* questions, as it turned out. If she'd known they would have to be secreted here under false pretenses, she would never have agreed to the trip.

Recalling this morning's fiasco in the cove, she felt more like a failure as a woman than ever. She had a feeling *that* encounter had everything to do with her restlessness. With a sigh, she lowered the comb to the dresser top, running her fingers through her shoulder-length brown hair. A rapping at her bedroom door startled her, and she spun around on the velvet bench. "Who is it?"

"It's the King of Mongo Pongo!" came a joking female voice. "Who do you think it is?"

Emily had to grin at her friend's banter. Slipping into a robe, she cinched the sash. "Okay, come in, Your Majesty."

The door burst open, and Meg rushed in, an intent expression on her pixie face. In pink shorts and matching top, she was fresh from the shower, her waist-length black hair pulled back into a still-damp braid.

"Thank goodness!" Meg barreled across the carpeted floor. "My room faces the heliport, so I saw the big chopper land, but I can't see the pool at all." Flinging open one of the tall windows, she dashed onto the balcony and leaned so far over the metal rail Emily worried that she might fall.

"What in the world are you doing?" She followed her friend to the door but didn't move any farther out when she noticed a crowd around the pool.

"I'm sure *he's* out there, and I'm determined to see him."

"Mr. Gallant?"

Meg straightened and leaned against the metal gridwork. "They're doing a photo shoot, and I heard Margo Tempest is going to be on the cover. So he must be down there. All those starlets? Where else would he be?"

Emily was confused. She'd heard of Margo Tempest, the newest Hollywood sensation,

but that was about all she could decipher from
Meg's ramblings. "What do you mean, photo
shoot?" Pulling her robe closer about her, she
dared a step onto the balcony to get a glimpse
of what was going on three stories below.

"You know, *Gallant's*!" Meg emphasized
that one word with a flourish of her arms,
apparently assuming that was explanation
enough.

Emily chanced another peek at the people
below. Sure enough, there were a dozen
shapely women down there, all clad in scanty,
see-through things. "Why, they're not even
dressed," Emily whispered, backing away
from the rail. She had an awful thought.
"What does Lyon Gallant do, anyway?" Meg
had mentioned he owned a catalogue
business. She'd pictured the periodicals she
received every few months like *Baxter's Seed
and Bulb Review* and *Mother Anderson's
Preserves*." Apprehensive, she clutched her
hands together. Why did she suddenly have
the feeling Lyon Gallant didn't sell anything
as tame as grape jelly or periwinkle seeds?

Meg laughed her deep laugh and shook her
head. "Emily, you amaze me. Don't tell me

you're the only woman in the world who doesn't get *Gallant's*! Good grief, you're more out-of-touch than I thought.'' She leaned over the balcony again. ''I see some men in suits, but I can't tell...*darn* that Lyon Gallant and his passion for privacy.''

Emily frowned, refusing to let the subject be changed. ''Just what does *Gallant's* sell? X-rated movies? If that *is* what he sells, then I'd just as soon not meet him.''

''That's the old, *dumped* Emily talking.'' Meg shook her head at her friend. ''Don't be such a prude.''

Emily's stomach clenched. ''Good lord. Then he *does* sell indecent movies?''

''Well, indecent, maybe, but movies? No.'' Meg's laughter was sharp and quick. ''Undies, Em. Expensive, indecent lingerie. *Gallant's* is such a sleek operation, movie stars and famous models fight to be photographed in it.''

As Emily absorbed this news, Meg twisted away and was bent nearly double, straining to see. ''Margo's the one in the red bustier and thong panties. Oh! *Oh!* There's a man in a beige sport coat that she's talking to. Tall, dark and to die for. I bet that's Lyon Gallant.'' She lurched up and motioned for Emily to come out, dropping her voice to a whisper. ''Emily, come here. I'm sure that's him.''

Emily had only been half-listening to her friend's gushing. ''He owns an *underwear* catalogue business?'' Relief rushed through her. Everybody wore underwear.

Meg guffawed again. ''Underwear? I guess *you'd* call it that. But nothing serviceable— not unless you have seduction in mind.'' Meg waved frantically, admonishing under her breath, ''Hurry, he's turning away.'' She was half hanging out over the balcony, one foot off the ground.

More in fear for her friend's safety than anything, Emily moved to the railing. ''Where?''

''Oh, darn!'' Meg popped back up, pointing. ''He went around behind those palm trees, onto the covered courtyard. Rats! Is it so much to ask that I see the man? Is that a sin?'' Without waiting for an answer, she bent over the railing, shading her eyes from the late afternoon sun.

"I guess not, but this *is* Sin Island," Emily reminded her, then had another disconcerting thought. "Why is it called—" She stopped herself. "Never mind. I don't want to know."

Meg's attention remained on the throng below. "It's not because of Mr. Gallant, if that's what you're afraid of. But considering his reputation with women, it could be. It's called Sin Island because it was a pirate hangout a couple of hundred years ago. Oh." She pointed frantically. "There's Margo again."

Emily watched as the starlet crawled onto the diving board and curled into a suggestive position. "Those panties can't be comfortable," she mused aloud.

"They're not for comfort, silly. They're for *sexy*." With a ponderous groan, Meg straightened and faced away from the photo shoot. "Oh, well, I guess he's gone. Darn! Do you suppose he'll join us for dinner tonight?"

"With Margo Tempest on the island?" She passed her pouting friend a doubtful look. "Who's being naive now?"

Meg shrugged and walked into the room. "I guess you're right." She plopped down on the bed. "But it's such a bummer to be in the same house with the world's most infamous playboy millionaire and never get to find out what he looks like. I promised a ton of people I'd get all the scoop."

Emily took a seat on the vanity bench. "Maybe it's better that we don't see him. I'd hate to have to look him in the eye and try to convince him I'm an interior decorator. I have trouble closing curtains, let alone designing them."

Meg made a face. "You worry too much. If he sees us, he'll probably just nod and be on his way. No problem. I only want to find out if he's as handsome as he's rumored to be."

Emily ran her hands through her hair again, absently fluffing the wet strands. "He probably looks like a thousand-year-old gnome with warts on his nose."

"Ha!" Meg retorted. "The man I saw by the pool was no warty gnome! If that was Lyon Gallant, he's as hot as . . ." The sentence died away, and the disgruntled scowl on her face began to alter into what looked like the beginnings of inspiration.

Emily experienced a tremor of misgiving. Meg had had some wild ideas in her twenty-six years, not all of them wise. As her smile bloomed, Emily had a sinking feeling this was going to be one of the wildest and least wise ideas of her life.

"I have it!" Meg jumped up. "He'd be perfect. Lyon Gallant could teach you everything you need to know about sex."

Emily stared, horror-stricken. Was it something about the sea air? Meg was voicing the exact thing she'd said to the carpenter this morning—the crazy fantasy of having a sexual encounter with Lyon Gallant. She wondered how many women a day got *that* insane notion, and since it seemed to be such a popular idea, how the secretive tycoon had time to get a lingerie catalogue out every month. "Don't even think it," she warned. "He wouldn't be interested in me."

Meg planted her fists on her hips. "Not the right attitude! You're every bit as pretty as Margo Tempest and a zillion times smarter. All you need is self-confidence."

"And maybe some of that painful underwear," she mumbled wryly.

"Exactly!"

Emily had turned away, but spun back. "No. Not if my life depended on it."

Meg's grin grew sly.

Emily loved the night. She loved walking in the moonlight, something she hadn't done in a long time. Tonight, she had a twofold reason to do it. First, Meg wouldn't shut up about the Lyon Gallant seduction foolishness. Second, well, it was basically the same reason. Meg was driving her crazy, forcing her to thumb through a *Gallant's* catalogue, oohing and ahing, over racy wisps of lace and silk that she insisted Emily *must* buy.

At her wit's end, she'd insisted she needed to take a walk, sure Meg wouldn't insist on tagging along. Her favorite show was about to start. As Emily headed outside, she thanked her lucky stars for Meg's passion for TV. Finally she'd get some peace. It was a beautiful June night. A light breeze teased her loose hair and carried on it the scent of tropical flowers and the salty tang of the sea. Palm trees waved their fronds as she crossed the manicured lawn, and stars winked from between scurrying clouds. Even the three-quarter moon seemed to be smiling at her.

She felt among friends. No one was lying, no one was cheating and no one was trying to get her to have sex with anybody else. That's what she loved about the night. Soft, quiet camaraderie. Her mood fell. Why couldn't she find that same quality in a man? Pushing the gloomy thought aside, she ambled along. It wasn't until it was too late that she became aware of where she was.

The cove!

What had possessed her to come here? She experienced a momentary discomfort but came to her senses. The obnoxious workman wouldn't be here now. It was too dark to work. He'd be in the employees' apartment compound on the far end of the island.

Feeling better, she strolled to the water's edge. The inky surface dipped and rose quietly, much of it lying in deep shadow. She was wearing tennis shoes and thought about taking them off and wading, but decided against it. One could never tell what lurked under the murky water. Still, it was a warm night, and a wade in the serene inlet seemed like a nice idea.

She tentatively stepped in with her shoes on, and the first cool sensations against her skin made her gasp. But she determinedly sloshed on until she was knee deep.

Her spirits lifted as the water caressed her legs. Nearing the halfway point, she noticed the sea had crept above her knees, so she stopped to roll up her walking shorts. She took a few more steps as water stole farther up her thighs, then found herself simply standing there. The vague white bones of the half-built cottage caught her eye. It perched above her, so silent, as though waiting to be turned into something lovely and valued.

"Like me?" she asked the night.

"I never said I didn't like you, sweetheart."

She was so startled by the deep, male voice coming from out of nowhere, she staggered. Unaccustomed to standing on sandy sea bottoms, especially encumbered by shoes, she lost her balance, and with a startled cry tumbled backward. She sputtered and flailed, trying to right herself. She knew the cove wasn't deep, but couldn't get her footing. She wasn't a good swimmer, and being startled, she floundered.

She felt a hand at her back, lifting her. She gagged, choked. The hand became an arm, supporting her shoulders until she could get her knees under her.

"Are you okay?" He was very near. His thigh brushed hers, so she knew he was either crouching or on his knees, too.

Coughing into her hand, she peered sideways at him. Her eyes stung and she wiped at them. "You scared me to death!" she rasped.

"I'm sorry." He grinned at her, the dim moonlight reflecting white teeth and a dreadful lack of remorse. His wide shoulders and lightly furred chest gleamed. The lower portion of his body was masked at belly level by rippling water. "I thought you saw me, since you were talking to me."

"I wasn't talking to you!" She winced, wishing she hadn't blurted that. She didn't want to explain her state of mind to this grinning hyena.

"Oh? Sorry." A brow rose. "Can you stand up?" His grin refreshed itself. "It seems like that's all I say to you."

She was affronted. "Are you suggesting I'm clumsy? You're the one booby-trapping the path and leaping out at me like a bogeyman."

He chuckled. "I've been busy today, haven't I?"

She knew she was overreacting again, but the residue of this morning's awful meeting still clung to her heart, making her feel defensive. Even in such dim light he was devilishly handsome. She didn't like to admit it, but he affected her—oddly. "Why are you here, anyway?" she demanded. "Don't you have a pool or a beach over at the employees' residence?"

He removed his arm from around her shoulders and backed away slightly, but didn't rise. "Both."

"Well—well, why are you out here in the dark?"

"Because I'm naked."

She'd opened her mouth to retort, thinking he was going to say something flip, like "I'm a loner," or "I hate crowds." But "I'm naked'' hadn't occurred to her. Her lips froze in a horrified oh.

His eyes twinkled. ''Were you going to say something?''

She swallowed, shaking her head. ''No— uh, no.''

''I thought you might suggest that since I'm already, shall we say, dressed for it, we could have sex.''

Her chest constricted and her breathing became labored. ''Uh—that was the farthest thing from my mind.'' That wasn't completely the truth.

''The farthest thing from your mind? What a shame,'' he said, his grin intact. She was appalled at how his blatant masculine appeal made her pulse race and her blood heat, even in the chilly water, yet when his sexual overture was refused, he didn't seem concerned—not even a little. She tried to bolt and run, but didn't seem to be able to stand. Her legs were tingly and unresponsive, especially the one he'd brushed with his thigh. She swallowed hard. At least that's what she *hoped* she'd brushed!

The water around them swelled and dipped. She was nearly breast deep in the water, but he was only covered to his waist. At most. The sea lapped, ebbed and flowed around them. One particular swell made the water dip dangerously low on his torso, and she blanched, tossing her gaze to the heavens where clouds scudded and the moon's grin had turned lecherous.

"See something interesting?" he asked.

She gritted her teeth at his taunting tone. "Don't you care that sometimes the water drops awfully low?" A salty wave smacked her cheek, splashing her hair, and she gasped at the impact. "Oh—that's a *big* one."

He chuckled. "Exactly what are we talking about?"

She swiped her sopping hair out of her eyes, counting to ten. She would not even respond to that! Maybe he was asking a straight question, but her mind wasn't on straight answers. *Darn her mind.*

Suddenly it occurred to her that her clothes were completely soaked, and she hunkered lower in the water to cover her breasts. Even if she did manage to bolt away, he'd be able to see every curve and—well, every curve when she stood up.

"I gather by now you've cut a deal for sex lessons with Mr. Gallant?"

The frank question stung. She drew her lips between her teeth but found herself nodding. It was the answer that required the least explanation. If she told him the truth—that she hadn't met Mr. Gallant, didn't want to meet the man, then Mr. Naked, here, would only tease her further with the idea of their having sex, since—as he'd so romantically put it— he was already dressed for it.

Unfortunately, there was one thing she'd discovered about being alone in a moonlit cove with a virile hunk. She was too much of a coward to simply have sex for the sake of sex. Darn her conventional hide. But there it was. The ugly truth. Meg would be livid if she found out!

"That was fast work," he said, with a scrutinizing quirk of his brow. "I hear Mr. Gallant's hard to meet. How'd you manage it?"

She didn't want to carry on this travesty one second longer. "Excuse me, but—I'm *wet*."

"No kidding." His brows dipped in mystification at her statement of the obvious.

She toyed with the top button of her blouse. "I mean, I'm *wet*," she repeated with firm emphasis. "This blouse is—is *thin*." She eyed him meaningfully. "I'd like to *leave*."

"That's fascinating."

Exasperated, she moaned, "Could you turn around?"

Dawn broke over his features, and he ran a hand across his lips, not masking his amusement too well. "Look, sweetheart, it's not like this is breaking new ground for me. I've seen women before. Wet and dry."

The idea that this naked stud was well-accustomed to the female anatomy made her body grow so warm she expected the water around her to give off steam. "Neverthe—" She stopped, cleared her throat of its shrill quality. "Nevertheless, I'd appreciate it if you'd turn around."

He didn't immediately comply, and his amused regard made her want to scream. Instead, she spat, "Mr. Gallant is expecting me." She bit the inside of her cheek, hating herself for such an unforgivable lie. It was just that the man tormented her so, it made her crazy!

His chiseled jaw lifted in a half nod, his gaze growing speculative. "Well, we can't make you late for class, now, can we?" The swish of water accompanied his turn. "How's this?"

"You're a prince," she shot, coming up on wobbly legs. "Good night."

"How will I know when it's safe to turn around?"

He was goading her! Always goading her! Clenching her fists, she shouted, "When you're a shriveled little thing."

He laughed outright, the sound low and sensual in the stillness. "That's a cruel thing to say to a naked man, sweetheart."

His wry comment made her stumble to a halt. Though he'd laughed, there was something about the lack of egotism in his remark that was endearing, and she felt an odd ambivalence spring to life. How ironic that one charming, almost vulnerable, statement could put a healthy crimp in her dislike for him.

Regaining her wits, she splashed to the far shore and hurried away. He'd probably just been trying to embarrass her. Still, the quivery sensation she'd experienced had nothing to do with the night breeze, and that was a shame.

How dare he be such a despicably irresistible exhibitionist!

Nearly a week later, Meg was still lathered up about the affair idea, and that was making Emily a nervous wreck. Mr. Gallant had been in and out the last several days, which hadn't helped her state of mind. What if he happened to cross their paths and they weren't in the west wing clambering around on ladders, shouting out measurements and nitpicking over just the right shade of puce for the settee?

Ivy had promised she'd alert them if that probability seemed imminent, but Emily couldn't help but feel, even with the housekeeper's assurance, something *had* to go wrong. As a matter of fact, she'd sensed a presence several times in the last few days, but when she'd turned she'd seen no one. She decided it was her guilty conscience getting the better of her.

Luckily, Mr. Gallant was a busy man and away most days and some nights. Regardless, she dutifully carried around her tape measure and her notepad, feeling like a fraud.

"Open up, Em! Hurry!"

Meg's frantic shout and her pounding on the door nearly caused the glass of water Emily had been drinking to slip from her fingers. She placed the stemmed crystal on her dresser and hurried to the bedroom door, expecting to see her friend's clothes on fire, considering the uproar she was causing. She flung the door wide. "What's wrong?"

Meg turned out to be completely intact, her white shorts and halter top not even singed. The only unusual thing about her was that she was waving an envelope. As soon as the door opened, she shoved it in Emily's face. "Read this!"

Out of self-defense, she took the beige note from her friend's quivering hand. "Why? What's so important?"

"It was under your door. I got one, too. Read it!" Her expression was so animated Emily was sure the news must be extraordinary. "What's happened?" She opened the flap of the envelope.

"Read! Read!" Meg's face was stained with color, and she looked as though she might burst from excitement.

"Okay, I'm reading." She unfolded the sheet of paper, but didn't have a chance to glance at it before Meg shouted, "Aloud! Read it aloud!"

Clearing her throat, she did as her friend asked. "Miss Emily Stone is invited to a formal dinner party in the Grand Salon at seven o'clock on Saturday evening. Sincerely, your host, Lyon Ga—" Her voice disappeared, and she blinked, hoping her eyes were playing ticks on her.

"Right!" Meg danced around like a kid, her voice a singsong of merriment. "Lyon Gallant has invited us to dine with him! Saturday night at seven!" She stopped frolicking and wheeled toward her friend. "Why do you suppose, after nearly two weeks, he's finally going to show himself to us?"

Emily was still staring at the note, but she'd heard Meg's question. Shaking her head, she folded it and unsteadily replaced it in its envelope. "I have no idea."

"Well, I don't care why. I'm just so excited I'll finally get to *see* him. Oh, and Aunt Ivy said there's this huge room around the corner with all kinds of evening gowns. We'll go pick out ours right after dinner. Now, let's see. This is Thursday. That means in only two days we'll see the master of Sin Island, up close and personal." She grabbed Emily's shoulders. "And, Em, this is your chance to meet him and—" she winked "—well, you know!"

"Meg, bite your tongue." Backing out of her friend's hold, she walked to her bed, tossing the invitation on it then dropping down heavily. "If you're my friend, you'll never mention that again."

"Don't go chicken on me," Meg cried. "Not with our goal in sight."

Emily felt a bouncy jolt indicating that Meg had plopped down beside her. She hadn't realized she'd closed her eyes and was rubbing them. But this whole subject was giving her a headache. Tiredly, she leaned back on her elbows. "Look, if I tell you something, will you promise to let this scheme of yours rest— for good?"

"Tell me what? I can't make a promise like that until I know what you're going to say." She crossed her arms, looking put out. "You could tell me something stupid, like the mating habits of fungus. And that wouldn't be fair."

Emily had to smile. "You didn't get much out of high school biology, did you?"

Meg grinned. "Why? Funguses don't mate? Well, then where do baby funguses come from, smarty?"

She sighed. "Will you be serious?"

Meg eyed her dubiously. "Okay. Talk. But I don't promise anything until I hear this."

Emily ran a hand through her hair, feeling scandalized. Unable to maintain eye contact, she allowed her gaze to rest on the distant ocean beyond the windows. It was a great silver beast, prowling beneath a sky that was giving off tempting glimpses of what would soon become another dazzling sunset. The day was perfection. So different from her mood. "Okay, here it is, straight out." She swallowed hard. "I asked a handsome island workman to have sex with me last week."

There was no response, not even a sound, for such a long time Emily couldn't help but peer at her friend. Meg was very still, her mouth hanging open. The sight of her sitting there, the image of a statue of a dental patient, was so comical she grinned in spite of herself.

"I don't believe it," Meg finally breathed. "So—so what happened with this blue-collar Adonis?"

Emily shrugged morosely. "To make a long story short—he said no. Then, that night, when he was naked—he offered to do it, but..." For some reason, the recollection made her jittery, and she lurched up, pacing to the window before she turned back. "I'm not going through that again."

Meg got up and moved to stand before her friend. "You asked a naked handyman to have sex with you?"

Emily nodded and stared out at the ocean. "Yes, and he turned me down flat—the first time. He wasn't naked then. Just made fun of me."

"I want to hear about the naked time!" her friend said, wonder in her tone.

"Well—he was up to his waist in water, but he was naked." She shook her head and moaned. "The point is, he wasn't really serious about having sex with me. He was just needling me." In a frail whisper, she admitted, "But—but he was so—so unbelievably good-looking. *If* he'd been serious, and *if* I ever could do such a reckless thing, it would be...with him." She leaned her forehead against the glass. It felt so frigid she knew she was blushing furiously. "Now, please promise me you'll never bring up the subject."

"Geez." Meg placed a consoling arm about Emily's waist. "Honey, you don't *ask* a man to have sex with you. You let him think it's *his* idea! Some sort of genetic macho thing makes them need to believe they're in charge. Smart women don't fight it, they *use* it." She patted Emily's arm. "You tell a man he's brilliant no matter what stupid thing he's talking about. Take his arm, and when you do, lightly brush your breast against him. You know— subtly show him you're hot to trot while pretending you hardly know he's alive. You can't be straightforward in the battle of the sexes, sweetie. It just isn't done!''

Emily was skeptical. ''It sounds deceitful to me.''

Meg shifted her around so they were face to face, and grinned. ''By George, I think you've got it! Now, since you've learned how *not* to do it, Auntie Meg is going to help you reel in the big fish.'' Hugging her, she declared, ''Look out, Lyon Gallant. Here we come.''

Icy dread knotted Emily's stomach. Meg hadn't heard a single word she'd said.

CHAPTER THREE

DARN that Lyon Gallant! Why had he decided to show himself after ignoring them for two solid weeks? Emily hadn't been able to concentrate on finding an evening gown after dinner. The large room had been full of formal clothes in all shapes and sizes by world-famous designers.

Meg almost hyperventilated from excitement, pulling gown after gown from the rack to take to her room and try on. But Emily's mind drifted to other things—dreadful things. Like being thrust into an unsuspecting Lyon Gallant's arms and expected to flirt him into bed.

She begged off with the excuse of a headache. Meg hardly noticed her departure, insisting she would pick out several gowns for her to try. Emily had a dire premonition Meg's choices wouldn't include floor-length, woolen monk's robes, but she wasn't up to worrying.

What she'd been dreading would happen in less than two days.

With no particular destination in mind— yet in the absolute opposite direction from the cove—she wandered across the manicured lawn, heading away from the mansion. After a few minutes she found herself in a meadow she'd passed many times that week on her new jogging route.

Under a waning moon, she could see the bobbing and nodding sea pinks and white-star rushes blooming among the meadow grasses. The sight was a balm to her frazzled emotions, and she inhaled the fragrant air, almost able to smile. Evening strolls had helped ease her spirits all her life. And even after her disastrous walk last week, she knew she'd made the right decision to come out tonight. Ever since the reminder of that cocky carpenter this evening, she'd felt jittery and upset, and needed some quiet time.

When she came to the edge of the meadow, the beach unfurled before her like a white ribbon. The surf whispered softly, caressing the bright sand like a lover's hand. That image made her uncomfortable. Determinedly she

shoved the notion aside, wanting to enjoy the
soft night without distressing thoughts.

Kicking off her loafers, she began to
shamble along, enjoying the feel of warm
sand between her toes. Going barefoot was
quite a deviation for her, and she grinned,
wondering if she should tell Meg about this
rash evolution in her behavior. "Emily," she
murmured, "you're a wild woman."

"Well, well. She smiles," came a male voice
Emily had never wanted to hear again. *It
was the carpenter.* She twisted around, but
couldn't immediately locate him. Her glance
fell on the only likely place he might be, a
cluster of live oaks ten or twelve feet ahead.

"Please don't tell me you're naked!" she
warned, hoarsely.

His chuckle was as vivid and thrilling as the
moonlight, but she tried to squelch her reaction. There was nothing about the workman
she cared to think of as thrilling. "That's no
answer!" She clenched her jaw, mortified to
be discovered out here, barefoot and talking
to herself—*again!* Why, oh, why did she have
to keep running into this guy?

She sensed movement as the man took shape, stepping out into the moon glow. Try as she could, she couldn't turn away. Her brain told her to close her eyes. What if he was naked? But her eyes remained open. Why couldn't she at least look somewhere else—at her feet, at the sky, anywhere? She managed only to lurch a defensive step backward.

"Satisfied, sweetheart?"

She blanched, her eyes as wide as platters. In this ghostly light, he seemed bigger, more virile than ever, and she felt threatened by that. His wide shoulders looked wider, and his craggy face was elegantly highlighted, skin taut over the prominent ridges of his cheekbones.

Uneasy, but helpless to stop herself, her glance dipped from his face, and she was greatly relieved to see damp swim trunks. The view of trim hips and long, powerful legs was still unsettling, even sheathed in wet cloth, so she hurriedly returned her gaze to his face. She was appalled to see moonlight glinting off a show of teeth. "You see, I'm not always naked."

Indignant, she scowled at him. "Just what do you do for laughs when I'm not around to harass?"

He began to walk toward her, his grin crooked. "Besides get naked?"

She inhaled shakily. "Could we change the subject?"

"Sure." He moved toward her with an amazing masculine grace for such a big man, reminding her of a roiling sea. Marvelous to look at, yet treacherous if you got in over your head. Silver moonlight poured over him, flaunting his muscular chest, his lithe torso. His long legs ate up the distance, strong thighs knotting and flexing as he came. "Let's talk about how the sex lessons are going."

Apprehension clutched at her, closing her throat. She wasn't sure if it was because she'd told him such a glaring lie, or that he was coming nearer. Wrapping her arms protectively about herself, she refused to give in to her panic and flee to the safety of the house.

Her heart thudded, but she stood her ground. Obviously he was heading in the opposite direction she was walking, and that was good. Her plan was to hurry by him and be on her way. With that decided, she felt more sure of herself. ''My sex life is none of your business.'' Pride forced her to add, ''But for your information, Mr. Gallant has been very—*very* helpful. Now, if you'll excuse me, I'm taking a walk.'' Managing to peel her arms from around her, she darted past him, resolving to put distance between them as quickly as possible.

''By coincidence, I was about to take a walk myself.'' He fell into step beside her.

She shifted to stare at him. ''But—you were going the other way.''

He grinned again. ''It's an island. What difference does it make which way I go?''

''Probably several hours, depending on where you want to end up,'' she muttered, then louder, ''I really wanted to be *alone*.''

''So, you're saying the reason I haven't seen you jogging this week is because you've found Mr. Gallant's lovemaking to be an adequate substitute?'' he asked, ignoring her unsubtle clue that she wanted him to go away.

Refusing to let him see how much the subject rattled her, she hedged. ''I hate to have to repeat myself, but my affair with Mr.

Gallant is none of your business." She chewed
the inside of her cheek, hoping he was buying
it. "Would you go *away*?"

"I've heard he's not much of a lover."
Dismayed by his audacity, she staggered to a
halt, swiveling to face him. "Compared to
some, that is," he finished, flashing her an
erotic grin.

"Like *you*, I suppose," she challenged,
though her pulse had begun to race wildly.
"You must have an astronomical trophy
room—full of blue ribbons for the biggest ego
in the universe." She whirled away, hurrying
along the beach. A sea turtle lumbered across
her path, and she leaped over it, wishing she
could as easily rid herself of another island
resident.

"What sensual things have you learned
from him?" he asked, sounding all too near.

"For one thing," she snapped, "I've
learned that gentlemanly behavior is more of
a turn-on than muscles, any day."

"Oh?" He sounded as though he was ab-
sorbing what she'd said. "So the owner of Sin
Island is a gentleman?"

"He's absolutely *charming*. If you need to go look up the word, don't let me stop you." She found herself warming to the lie. This man needed his ego pricked. Why not enjoy herself while she did the females of the world a service? "As a matter of fact, I don't believe I've ever met anyone more charming than Lyon!"

"I've been told I'm charming."

"Ha!" she jeered. "Some activists say the ozone layer is just peachy, too."

"You're comparing me to a gigantic toxic hole?"

"It's not much of a stretch."

His laugh was quick and rich. "I hope the ozone layer is properly flattered."

Emily found herself having to bite her lip to keep from smiling at his dry wit. Irritated with herself, she quickened her pace. The last thing she wanted was to start enjoying this man's company. In a desperate effort to get him to leave her alone once and for all, she threw back, "Your ego is probably what caused the damage to the ozone layer in the first place."

"Those poor, innocent fluorocarbons," he said. "Because of me, they've taken such abuse."

Her breathing was coming unevenly from her exertion. Why wasn't this man winded? She refused to allow herself to dwell on just how he stayed in shape. Wanting to say something pithy, she opened her mouth to retort, but decided she needed all her air just to stay alive.

"This isn't jogging anymore. This is sprinting," he cautioned, amusement in his voice.

"Drop...out anytime." She huffed and puffed, gulping air. "I wouldn't...want to put a crimp in...your sex life."

"Speaking of sex," he said, "what has he taught you so far?"

She couldn't believe her ears. Before she registered what she was doing, she was standing still, glaring. *"What?"* It came out as a wheeze through a painful intake of air.

He shrugged. "I think I was clear."

"Clear?" she echoed, incredulous. "Let's search a little farther for a better word for what you are.'' She paused to inhale. ''What about *rude*?'' ,

''I think you're lying.'' His eyes sparked with mockery. ''I don't think you've even met Lyon Gallant.''

''I *have*!''

''Then show me what he's taught you.''

She sputtered, panicked by his challenge. ''Why should you care? Since he's such a mediocre lover!''

''I'm curious about your opinion.'' He scanned her face, his lids half-lowered. ''Did he teach you a sexy way to kiss?''

His question was seductive, and she shuddered involuntarily, startled at herself. She'd never had such a sensual reaction to a simple string of words before.

His moonlit expression was deliciously appealing, so much so that when she opened her mouth she was unable to form a scathing response.

''Show me.''

The soft dare affected her badly—with a mixture of fear and desire and something very akin to heart failure. One corner of his mouth quirked in a half-grin, and she knew he sensed her quandary. "I hate to repeat myself, too," he prodded. "But I don't believe you've met him."

His continued taunts, and even worse, his incredulity that she could possibly interest a man like Lyon Gallant, were like tossing twig after twig on the small flame of her pride. She'd never been a proud or boastful person, but this man had thrown so much fuel onto the small flicker that suddenly it exploded into an inferno. She would *not* allow him to back her into a corner, make her admit she had no idea how to kiss seductively. Her self-esteem had been seriously damaged by Harry's desertion, and she couldn't stand another humiliation.

She made a silent pledge to dismember this workman if he even made eye contact with her again while she was stuck on this island. "If I show you *one* thing, will you go away and leave me alone? Never mention sex or Lyon Gallant again? As a matter of fact, never *speak* to me again?"

His answer was a low chuckle.

"Not good enough."

"Would that be the gentlemanly thing to do?"

She lifted a mutinous chin. "It would."

His teeth gleamed in the dim light, a breathtaking sight. "I thought you said I was no gentleman."

She reached out and poked his chest, registering the tightly drawn skin too thoroughly. Stiffening, she dropped her hand, rubbing away the feel of him. "Try," she warned. "Try very hard."

"Fair enough." He nodded. "Now, the sexy kiss."

For the briefest instant she swayed between a feminine longing to know the taste of those lips and a desire to slap his face. A thought flashed in her brain and she immediately saw her salvation. "I didn't say it would be a kiss."

His eyes narrowed, but she ignored the tempest she'd set to brewing there. With as little physical contact as possible, she took his arm. "To show a man you're—available..." She faltered, struggling to recite Meg's lesson from earlier in the evening. "You take his arm." She wrapped her arm about his with grudging reluctance. "Then—then you press him lightly against your breast." Without demonstrating the pressing part, she let go. "Now that that's settled, have a nice life." Tossing him an acrimonious glance, she headed down the beach.

The hand on her elbow came as such a shock she couldn't react. In less than a heartbeat, she was hauled against a firm chest, her mouth devoured by hot, coaxing lips. The effect was dizzying, and the world slid sideways on its axis. It was lucky for Emily that strong hands were holding her, keeping her from falling off the edge of the precariously tilted planet.

Her eyelashes fluttered against his cheek as she tried to make sense of a world that had been severely damaged. Her numbed mind registered the fact that she was hugging his neck for dear life. Slowly, she became aware of the splendor and strength of the man holding her in his arms, and of the fact that she was not caught up in the vortex of some cataclysmic earthquake. She was being kissed with such mastery her senses were reeling out of control, her emotions wildly spiraling and tumbling.

His lips were hard and searching, yet surprisingly gentle. She felt a heady sensation of delight, and startled herself by relaxing fully against him. An unruly longing had been building inside her ever since the night in the cove, a gnawing hunger she was surprised to discover she even possessed. But with the touch of his lips and his knowing hands, it raged out of control. 'Certainly, no kiss or caress she'd ever shared with Harry had sent the pit of her stomach into a spin the way this overconfident carpenter's did.

Or possibly, her mind argued, *he isn't all that overconfident. The man knows how to kiss!*

His mouth moved across hers, sending a honeyed heat through her veins like no heat she'd ever experienced. Sweet yet suggestive, the message in his lips made her breath come in short gasps and her legs as tenuous as threads. She sighed against his lips, her fingers snaking up to luxuriate in his silky hair. The man's kiss was gloriously clever in the ways of seduction, and she found herself slipping toward surrender.

His hands, which had begun a stirring exploration of her back, were suddenly holding her face, his lips lifting away from hers. A moan of regret escaped her throat, and she reached for him, not wanting the kiss to end, but he stepped away. Before he completely relinquished her face, he brushed her lips with one lingering finger.

She stared, feeling drugged. His face was indistinct, and she wondered if his kiss had struck her blind. She blinked, casting her gaze to the sky. The moon was nothing more than a glossy smudge behind a scudding cloud.

"My compliments to your tutor," he murmured, his voice vaguely rough. She glanced at his face, still hidden by deep shadow. She couldn't see his expression, couldn't tell if his eyes were glinting with mockery. Was he making fun of her again? Of course he was. She would have to be an idiot to believe otherwise. *He'd* done all the kissing, and he knew it. How dare he be so unkind!

In a self-protective move, she lifted a hand to her passion-swollen lips to mask their trembling. "That was shabby behavior—" her voice broke and she had to struggle to finish "—even for you." Fighting tears, she tore off toward the house as though the devil himself was nipping at her heels.

Emily stood staring at herself in the dresser mirror, for the first time noticing how tan she'd gotten during these past two weeks. Of course, the ivory color of her long gown made her skin seem more burnished than it really was. She wasn't accustomed to seeing her skin so golden-brown. And though it wasn't particularly good for the skin, she now understood why people actively sought a tan. It gave the skin an ironically healthy glow.

She ran a finger along the ridge of a cheekbone, shaking her head at herself. The fresh dusting of freckles made her look eighteen again. Another irony struck her. She hadn't worn a formal dress since she'd been that age, when her father had won Plattville, Iowa's teacher of the year award.

She sighed, remembering how the occasion had been marred by the fact that her sister, Elsa, had run away to New York only a few weeks before, breaking her father's heart. Since her mother had died three years earlier, Emily had gone as her father's escort. He hadn't been able to fully enjoy the honor because of his oldest daughter's defection. And even though Emily had done her best to be a cheerful companion, she would never forget the pall that had hovered over *that* formal occasion.

This dress, however, was a far cry from the childish, pink, puffed-sleeve garment she'd borrowed from a neighbor. This silk creation looked more like a nightgown than anything that should be worn in mixed company. It clung to her breasts, her hips, and the slit up the side revealed more leg than most of her walking shorts.

Still, this had been the best of the lot Meg had brought for her to try. Besides, with the hip-length flared jacket, it was respectable. She only hoped it would be cool enough in the Grand Salon for her to keep the jacket on all evening. Otherwise, she'd simply have to leave early. There was no way she was taking off her jacket in public.

Glimpsing her watch, she confirmed her fear that it was nearly seven o'clock. With one last, critical look at her sun-streaked hair, combed straight back and fastened with a pearl-encrusted clip at her nape, she picked up the jacket and slid it on, fastening the single button at her waist. She had to admit it was an elegant formal suit. The jacket alone must be worth thousands of dollars, for the bodice and collar were trimmed in satin and lace and embellished with pearls.

Meg had insisted on the pearl hair clip, but Emily had refused to borrow earrings. All this borrowing of finery only reminded her of her sister's desertion—and then her sudden re-appearance, coming back for their father's funeral, lingering just long enough to lure Harry away...

Emily's glance veered from her stricken reflection. Instead of attending this starched dinner party, she wished she could go off alone and sit on a secluded beach. Except there was always the danger of running into that disturbing carpenter and his equally disturbing kisses.

Her mood darkened with worry. She supposed accepting the hospitality of their aloof host for the past two weeks had to be paid for in whatever manner he required. She only hoped his other guests would occupy his time and he wouldn't ask them how the remodeling of the west wing was going. Surely there would be enough starlets at the dinner to keep their host occupied. She was a bad liar, and she knew, if cornered, she'd blurt out, "I'm a no-good fraud! Send me to prison!" That would be horrible for Ivy.

As she picked up her satin bag, preparing to go to Meg's room, there was a knock at her door.

"Meg?" she asked.

"Yes, it's me in all my fancy gewgaws. I only wish Larry could see me. He'd ravage me right here in the hall."

Emily managed a smile. Meg's bubbly humor was one of the greatest gifts she gave to their friendship. "Maybe it's better that he's in Brazil, then." She tried to picture Meg's bashful, bespectacled husband as a sex machine, but had a hard time. "I'm not sure I'm ready to see Larry in his ravaging mode."

The door opened and in flounced Meg. She was stunning and sexy, the shimmering image of a diminutive Cher, especially with all that hair, a cascade of black gold falling nearly to her waist. She wore a short, skintight dress made of crushed peacock-blue sequins. A matching sequined pouch with a satin cord dangled from one of her outstretched arms. "Ta da!" she sang. "Am I not wonderful?" She did a full turn, and the light caught the sparkle of a rivulet of impressive, square-cut diamonds hanging from each ear. "Am I not too-too?"

Emily smiled a real smile, feeling better in the face of Meg's enthusiasm. "You're very too-too. As a matter of fact, you're the most too I've ever seen."

Meg laughed that deep laugh of hers. "If Mr. Gallant looks even half as svelte in his tux as I look in this dress, I'll eat my purse."

"He couldn't possibly," Emily said, meaning it. When Meg tried, she was one of the most striking people she'd ever seen. "Nobody will be able to hold a candle to you."

"I'm afraid I must agree." Meg tossed her head in mock haughtiness. "But don't put yourself down. Why, because of my great eye for clothes, you're almost as gorgeous as I am." Taking Emily's hand, she tugged her to the door. "Let's us two gorgeous people get going. I'll burst if I don't see Mr. Gallant in the next five minutes. And I know you're dying to meet him, too." She winked wickedly. "Aren't you?"

Emily bit the inside of her cheek, drawing blood.

The parquetry dining room table was as long as a bus, making even the twenty-five people clustered at one end seem like a very small party.

The meal proved to be the most spectacular gourmet spread Emily could have imagined. The only flaw in the grand affair was that it was taking every ounce of her strength to keep Meg from leaping up and bodily strangling the butler, who kept coming in every fifteen minutes to explain that Mr. Gallant would be delayed a bit longer.

Meg had never been long on patience. Neither had she mastered the art of taking disappointment well. So she was fit to be tied. And the glaring evidence of their host's vacant place at the head of the table was a galling reminder of how desperately she'd looked forward to meeting the mysterious master of Sin Island.

In a valiant effort to keep Meg's mind diverted from murder and mayhem, Emily struggled to keep the conversation flowing. She was someone who hardly ever initiated a conversation, and her efforts were laborious and stressful. The evening seemed to be passing in harrowing slow motion.

Another unfortunate thing about the evening was that there were no starlets in attendance. Besides Emily and Meg, the entire party consisted of the accounting department of *Gallant's* and their spouses. It was explained by the executive vice president of accounting, Albert Benton, that Mr. Gallant gave an appreciation dinner for each of his departments at some point during the summer months.

Albert was a quiet widower in his mid-forties, and he assured Emily and Meg they were delighted to have fresh faces at their traditional dinner, more opportunity for interesting discussions. That comment had sent panic rampaging through her. She and Meg were supposed to be interior decorators, and they knew nothing about the subject. How could they add anything interesting when they didn't know anything—at least not about decorating? Consequently, there were huge gaps in conversation. It became obvious very quickly that *Gallant's* accountants and the two pseudo-decorators didn't have much to say to each other.

One of the accountants, a divorced man named Farnley Morse, was a hard-nosed Trekkie in his off-duty hours. Whenever he grabbed the reins of the conversation, it moved into outer space, to Spock, Captain Kirk, three-eyed androids and all manner of inter-galactic angst. These were subjects that bored Meg to distraction and could only incite her to grimmer, more bloodthirsty thoughts of homicide. So Emily had the additional tribulation of steering Farnley away from a subject that was close to his heart and clearly always on the tip of his tongue.

After almost an hour, Emily found herself thanking heaven for the three college students, Claude, Lester and Reed, who were summer employees of the Gallant company. At first they'd been quiet and seemed as uncomfortable as Emily, but after awhile they'd gotten over their awe of the place and turned into real assets. Between them, they were keeping the guests laughing over stories of one campus prank after another.

When one topic faded, Emily would jump in, stabbing at any subject that came to mind that didn't include death, stars or thoughtless hosts, hoping the animated young men would come to the rescue again.

She checked her watch. Eight-thirty. The last remnants of the delicious crabmeat chantilly had been cleared away, and almost everyone was through with dessert. She lowered her gaze to what was left of her poached pears with gingered cream, praying this ordeal would come to an end soon.

Just then, the butler made another of his dreaded appearances, and all conversation halted. It seemed to Emily that the guests were holding their collective breaths.

The formally clad servant cleared his throat. "If you would care to retire to the patio, there is a small orchestra setting up for your dancing pleasure."

Meg raised her hand and waved a napkin at the butler as he was about to go. "Wait a second," she called, her face puckered in a frown.

"Yes, madam?" He returned to a position of respectful attention.

"Is Mr. Gallant joining us there?"

"I couldn't say, madam," he replied, a model of the noncommittal manservant. "Now, if you will follow me?"

Meg's fist tightened around her dessert fork, and Emily patted her hand. "Easy, tiger. Mr. Gallant will show up." Secretly, she doubted it, didn't even want it to be true. And though she wouldn't say it, deep inside, she was harboring a burgeoning resentment for a host who could be this inconsiderate.

Once outside, Emily noticed the night air was unusually still and close, as though it, too, was holding its breath in anticipation of something. She chewed her lower lip. Her jacket would soon become uncomfortably warm, especially if she did much dancing. Since the men outnumbered the women this evening, the chances were good that she'd have to take her share of spins around the floor.

She turned at the sound of stringed instruments tuning up, surprised their absent host had hired an orchestra. The idea of airlifting twenty-odd musicians to his island home boggled her mind, and she shook her head. The extravagant way Mr. Gallant lived continued to amaze her.

She knew the big helicopter made daily trips back and forth to the mainland. Some days several. And today it had come and gone three times that she knew of. She wondered if Mr. Gallant had left the island and hadn't returned. Or possibly he'd left, then returned while they were at dinner. Maybe he was changing, preparing to join them now. She had no idea where he was and didn't much care, except for the fact that Meg was dying a lingering and painful death from curiosity.

The orchestra began to play "Red Sails in the Sunset." As couples took to the floor, she strolled to the edge of the terrace and leaned against the metal railing, staring out to sea. Off in the distance she saw shimmering threads of lightning rip through the black fabric of sky. A storm was brewing. She smiled wanly. There was a storm brewing much, much closer at hand—Hurricane Meg! She closed her eyes, hoping Mr. Gallant wouldn't be a complete cad, that he would show himself before much longer. Just a glimpse would be enough. For Meg's sake.

The music changed. This time, it was an orchestration of Billy Joel's latest hit. She couldn't recall the name, but she liked the beat.

"Emily?" came a tentative male voice a second before someone leaned against the railing at her side.

She turned, already knowing it was Claude. Thin as a wafer, with a shock of woolly red hair that looked as though it perpetually needed sheering, he stood there, trying but failing to look casual. She'd had a feeling all through dinner that he was developing a schoolboy crush on her, and her heart went out to him. "Hi, Claude." She smiled amiably. "Wasn't dinner nice?"

"Great. Uh..." He looked nervous. Though he was a year or two older than her high-school students, he seemed very young and vulnerable. If he was afraid she might reject his offer to dance, he was wrong. Her own heartache had been too recent for her to bear to see even a glimmer of disappointment in anyone's eyes because of her. Though the night was overly warm, she decided she would endure it with a smile. She'd learned all too well how fragile the human heart was—and how easily it could be trampled. Harry and Elsa had shown her that.

"I was just wondering if you'd like to..." His question died away, and she sensed he was distracted by something behind her. Curious, she turned in the direction he was looking and instantly saw what it was. All eyes had gravitated to a remote, princely figure, silhouetted in burnished light that spilled from the open double doors of the mansion.

Emily got only a peek at the newcomer as the guests converged around him. Still, she was left with a definite impression of a lean yet powerfully built man clad in formal black. Could this be their elusive host who had finally arrived at his own party? Her stomach clenched in panic.

"Hey," Claude said. "I bet that's Mr. Gallant."

Emily saw another flash of lightning, this one almost overhead, and felt a sudden breeze that carried the scent of rain. A storm was coming, and would be quickly upon them. Claude's comment registered belatedly. "Haven't you met him, either?"

"Nah. He doesn't get to accounting much. And I've only been there since classes let out in May." His expression grew hesitant and he said something, but thunder swept away the sound. "Think we should go meet him?" he repeated, after the rumbling died down.

"Maybe we should wait and see if the others survive."

He did a double take, then understood she was joking, and laughed. "Yeah, I guess that was a stupid question."

She shifted to watch the activity at the other end of the patio, and was startled to see a small group of people separating themselves from the crowd and moving her way. Meg was chatting animatedly with a very tall man who must be their host. Her heart went to her throat. Surely she wasn't dragging Mr. Gallant over there specifically to meet her? *Please, Meg,* she cried silently. *Please be talking about the wonderful dinner or the softness of the guest towels! Anything, as long as it has nothing to do with sex lessons!*

She knew she was panicking. Even Meg wouldn't do anything so crazy. She tried to buck up, to get control of herself, and pasted on a sociable smile. It was finally time to meet her shadowy host, and it wouldn't be good form for her to scream and bolt over the patio railing just because he made a move to shake her hand.

She forced her gaze from Meg's face. Even if the light had been better, she couldn't read lips. She could only trust in her friend's basic good sense and assume all was well.

Claude surprised her by stepping in front of her like a protective puppy. He introduced himself first, making polite comments about how delighted he was to be an employee and a dinner guest. Emily took the opportunity to scan the sky again. Clouds had blown in and shrouded the stars and moon. Darkness seemed to be pressing down around them, dank and ominous. Thunder growled through the heavens, and she couldn't hear Mr. Gallant's response. It didn't really matter, but the coming storm did. Any second now a torrential rain would start to fall.

There was a shuffle of feet and she sensed Claude moving away. Meg interjected, "Last but not least, Mr. Gallant. This is Emily Stone, my, er, fellow decorator."

Here it came, the big lie! She tried not to show her dismay, and extended her hand. "How do you do, Mr.—"

Lightning exploded above them, turning the night into stark, brilliant day. It was only an instant, but long enough for Emily to freeze in naked horror. That knowing look, that roguish grin, high amusement in a dusky gaze. It was all so distressingly familiar.

He stood there grinning at her, looking sophisticated and flawless in a tuxedo. She didn't want to believe her eyes and blinked several times, hoping it was a trick of the lightning storm. But, when she looked again, he was still there.

"You..." she breathed, wishing the earth would open up and swallow her, or that a hurricane would sweep her away into oblivion. She'd actually thought he was a carpenter—a cocky, arrogant handyman—and she'd told him...told to him she was having an affair with—*with*...

She became aware of a commotion around them, noticed big, fat drops of rain had begun to fall as guests scrambled for cover. But she didn't move, couldn't care less about something so inconsequential as deadly lightning slashing around them. Her eyes grew wet with anger and humiliation. "How dare you!" She jerked up her arm to give him the hardest, most well-deserved slap any man had ever received in the history of the world.

"Would you care to take my arm?" He caught her uplifted hand before she could follow through with her urge. "When marble gets wet, it's treacherous."

"That—that's not the only treacherous thing on the island!" She tried to wrench free, but he held her fast. What a diabolical joke he'd played, egging her on then kissing her the way he had. She yanked on his hold again, but it did no good. Loathing shook her, and she cried, "I'd rather be torn limb from limb by a pack of rabid dogs than touch you!"

"I must insist." Slipping her arm around his, he imprisoned her against him. Iron-hard muscle nudged her breast, and she inhaled sharply at the contact. "It would be the gentlemanly thing to do. Don't you agree—sweetheart?" His low query was rich with lazy laughter.

CHAPTER FOUR

THUNDER, like a snarling bear, accompanied them as they entered the Grand Ballroom. Servants scurried to close doors and help the orchestra set up. But because Emily was clutched so securely to her host, her roiling emotions didn't allow her to register much activity.

"Are you still interested in having a wild, sexual affair with the owner of Sin Island, Miss Stone?" he asked near her ear.

She flashed him a dismayed look. "Let go of me!"

He shrugged his wide, exquisitely clad shoulders, and she was mortified that she could feel it in her breasts. "Answer my question first," he cautioned.

"Maybe you haven't been keeping up, Mr. Gallant. I loathe you and I hope never to lay eyes on you again!"

He grinned. "I'd love to dance, thanks."

Before she could deny him, he'd swept her into his arms. It wasn't until that moment that she noticed the orchestra had recovered itself and had struck up the sultry ballad, "When a Man Loves a Woman." He drew her against him with menacing resolve, forcing her body familiarly to his. She gasped, then couldn't breathe at all. "We can start with how to dance seductively," he murmured, his breath warm against her temple.

"We can start with my knee in your groin," she warned, her voice strained.

He chuckled, his big hand spanning her waist, drawing her more firmly against him. Her nerves leaped and shuddered as his body moved against hers, scandalizing her with subtle misdeeds. She knew he was daring her to make good on her threat, but she couldn't. She couldn't even talk.

She fought for air. It was stifling. Were they in a cave or a vault? She cast her gaze around. The room was large and airy. Though the many chandeliers were only dimly glowing, she could tell the room was white but for the golden veins in the marble floor and the gilded columns that stood like palace sentinels between tall windows. There had to be plenty of oxygen in the huge ballroom, so why couldn't she breathe?

Lightning flashed outside the windows, and thunder boomed, rattling the glass. A wind-tossed storm was battering the island, but nature's violent tumult was puny compared to Emily's state of mind. She tried to concentrate on drawing deep breaths, to get her mind away from the bold feel of him, but it was no use. His touch, his scent, triggered unfamiliar longings deep inside her.

A rebellious voice chided, *Remember his kiss, Emily? Why not throw caution to the wind? Take him up on his offer!* Hadn't she discovered the hard way that people who succeed in life are those who grab for what they want? Didn't she learn that lesson when her sister stole Harry from her? Elsa was always competitive. It was clear she'd decided she wanted what Emily had, and she just took it. So, what was she hesitating for? This gorgeous man was offering her lovemaking lessons. Who was she to deny herself?

"You're doing very well." His low assurance drew her from her troubled thoughts.

She jerked to look at his face, stunned that he would say such a thing. He was grinning crookedly; a dimple slashed one cheek. She was sure he was making fun of her, for she was a poor dancer. Harry had despaired of teaching her the simplest of steps. "Must you ridicule me *all* the time?"

He lifted a speculative brow. "I thought I was complimenting you."

She frowned, baffled. Then it dawned on her. She was *dancing* with him—close, even intimately! Her hips moved in concert with his. Their legs were brushing and rubbing rhythmically, and she hadn't once tromped on his feet. Her breasts had somehow pressed themselves against his chest. She even had an awful feeling her head had been cuddled in the crook of his neck before he'd brought her out of her musings.

Oh, lord! He was not only an expert kisser, but a wonderful dancer—able to lead her, guide her, make her feel as though she, too, could dance. But there was a negative side to that talent, a side that was becoming clear to her for the first time in her life. A truly clever man could actually make love to a woman on a dance floor. Lyon Gallant was distressingly clever in that regard, for he had wordlessly, deliberately drawn her toward surrender in a matter of only a few minutes—with all his clothes on and in the middle of a room full of people!

She swallowed hard, fighting to preserve her sanity. "You've had your dance. Now please go away." It had been hard to string that many stern words together without a break in her voice, but she managed. The music changed to a samba, and she lifted her chin to reiterate her demand.

"But, Miss Stone, we've only begun our lessons." His gaze exuded confidence in his ability for wild fulfillment, and her heart stumbled over a beat.

"I really believe you'd go through with it. I also believe it doesn't matter to you one way or the other." She pushed at his chest and freed herself from his embrace, working to reinforce her anger. But her mortification at the cruel trick he'd played on her over-powered her hostility, and she had to ask, "Why did you—" Though they were no longer touching, the intensity of his gaze was unnerving, and a waver in her voice betrayed her. Valiantly, she went on, "Why did you lie to me about who you were?"

His brows rose in question. "Lie?"

"You told me you *worked* for Mr. Gallant!"

He shrugged his hands into his tux pockets, looking princely and unconcerned. "I told you nothing, sweetheart. You assumed all that."

"You let me!" she charged. "That's just as bad!"

He studied her leisurely. Lightning flashed and lit a fire in his eyes, a breathtaking sight. "To be honest, it irritated me that you fabricated an affair with—me." At last he smiled, but the amusement was minimal. "Do you really blame me?"

That stopped her, and she clamped her jaws shut. There was nothing she could say to redeem herself. She had lied. Not only that, she was *still* lying. He thought she was an interior designer. She hated herself for that, but couldn't do a thing about it. Ivy's job depended on her keeping that secret. She felt a creeping, sickening unease in her stomach.

She was caught, both in the lie he knew about and the one she hoped he would never discover.

She peered at him. "Okay, okay. Let's call it even and never speak to each other again."

"Even?" She flinched at his sardonic repetition of the word. "What did I do to you, except offer you what you asked for?"

She felt a whisper of desire rush through her at the reminder, but squelched it. "I'll tell you what you did! You kissed me against my will!"

He was silent for a long moment, his narrowed gaze appraising. She grew nervous in the extended quiet, but she was also filling up with an odd sense of excitement. It was hard to dwell on that kiss and remain untouched by the memory. "If I'm not mistaken," he reminded softly, "you kissed me back."

She sucked in an offended breath. "And— and I thought he—you were a gentleman!" She nearly choked on the word. Spinning on her heel, she dashed away, vowing never again to set foot in the same room with Lyon Gallant as long as she was stuck on his island.

After lurking in one of the sumptuous bathrooms until she felt like a silly schoolgirl, Emily entered the ballroom. Though the lights were low, it was a glittery, festive place full of music and laughter—except for the shadow that surrounded Emily's heart.

People were dancing or standing around the refreshment table and visiting. She could see Lyon waltzing with one of his accountant's wives. He was smiling as she chatted. Always the striking, perfect host. Meg was nearby, her dress sparkling like blue fireworks as she danced with shy Claude.

Sighing wanly, Emily scanned the double doors. They were flung wide, a rain-freshened breeze blowing in. Apparently the storm passed while she was in hiding. Making her way around the edges of the gathering she went out onto the patio and inhaled the storm-cooled air. It refreshed her spirits and she made her way to the far end of the patio. Scurrying down a set of steps that curved away from the house, she entered an unlit garden. Everything twinkled under a cascade of moon glow.

Her glance moved from the lavish plantings toward the house. The Gallant mansion was an imposing, three-story residence nestled in the brow of a hill. Even as ultramodern as the buff, terra-cotta structure was, it had a classic formality about it that was dramatic, juxtaposed against the succulent tropical landscape that cradled it.

From aboard the helicopter the day she'd arrived, it had been vaguely reminiscent of an Egyptian temple or some stark, walled monastery. Yet, upon closer inspection, Emily had discovered its architecture was strikingly modern. Unbidden, her thoughts veered to her host. His home seemed to reflect his personality. Contemporary yet classic, daring yet aloof.

She spun away, wanting to laugh bitterly. He was aloof, all right, unless you happened to run into him under the moon. Then he was—he was . . .

She bit her lip, not caring to think about what he was. *Exciting, sensual, hard to resist.* Though many bothersome descriptions flitted through her mind, aloof was not among them.

Not when he'd spent all their time together teasing and insulting her.

Noticing the moon's reflection in a small pond in the center of the lush garden, she felt a blow to her stomach. *The moon!* Lyon always seemed to be popping out at her in the moonlight. Though she'd just seen her host inside, she couldn't trust him as long as she stood under a moon—couldn't trust herself. Maybe she was safer inside. Even better, maybe she should escape to her room.

As she ran up the steps, she almost slammed into Meg. "Oh, there you are!" Her friend took her shoulders to balance them both. "I've been looking everywhere." Her smile was victorious. "I have some juicy dish about why Mr. Gallant was late tonight."

Emily blinked at her friend, not caring to hear this, but knowing that interrupting when she was enthusing on a subject was worthless.

"This is the deal. According to one of the maids, Mr. Gallant was visiting Belinda Bane, the glamorous movie star, in her Colorado hideaway, negotiating for her to appear in his catalogue. Bad weather prevented him from flying out when he'd planned." She stopped to take a breath, giving Emily a sly look. "And don't we all know what *negotiation* means when it comes to Lyon Gallant and beautiful women?" She didn't wait for Emily to ponder that. "It means hot, wild sex!"

Emily's stomach clenched.

Meg squeezed her shoulders. "Speaking of that, you did really well in there, Em. I could tell he was interested. But why are you out here? Playing hard to get?"

"Oh, Meg..." Emily moaned, unable to push from her mind the image of Lyon Gallant and the leggy superstar entwined in silken sheets. "That man would be interested in a fence post if you put a skirt on it."

Meg's smile faded. "What's wrong with that? You aren't looking to marry the guy, just to *learn* from him!"

"I've decided there's nothing I want Mr. Lyon Gallant to teach me."

Meg dropped her hands and took a step back, looking as though she'd been hit. "What's the matter? Is he—weird? Did he want you to do kinky stuff, like join him in a threesome or something?"

Emily winced, feeling a headache coming on. "Of course not. He's just—just too—too..." She shook her head, at a loss for words.

"Too what?"

"I don't know." She felt like a fool. What was wrong? Why couldn't she simply jump into a brief fling with the man and enjoy it? "Too cavalier, I guess."

Meg exhaled theatrically, eyeing heaven. "I don't get you, sweetie. Here we've done the impossible and you have one of the hunkiest men in America interested in having sex with you, and you don't want to because he didn't barf at the idea?"

"But—but to think he's jumping from Belinda Bane's bed to mine then to somebody else's. It seems so—so..."

"How do you think he became an expert? Self-help sex books?" Meg clamped her hands on her hips. "Try to forget any fairy-tale ideas about lovemaking having to be connected with commitment. This is reality, sweetie! And your reality needs work!"

No matter that Meg was trying to help, that observation hurt. "You talk so big, but I bet

Larry wasn't any wild sex maniac when you met him.''

Meg giggled. "Don't underestimate the quiet type.''

"I'm the quiet type.''

"You're quiet *and* inhibited. Not a good combo.'' She grasped Emily by the shoulders again and shook her slightly. "Focus, Em. Let Lyon Gallant be your teacher. You'll learn from an expert. Then, when your true love comes along, you'll have the ammo to shoot him down.''

"Enchanting metaphor.''

Meg made a face. "I hate it when you toss your vocabulary at me.'' Snatching her by the hand, she began dragging Emily toward the ballroom. "Now, get in there and learn!''

Emily balked. "No, I'm going to my room.''

Meg stopped, eyed her friend, then nodded curtly. "You could be right. Make him yearn for you.''

Emily sighed. "Fine. Whatever. Good night.''

Meg stuck out a thumbs-up sign and winked. "It's you and me, sweetie, all the way."

Rain fell all day, and Meg and her aunt were ensconced in Ivy's quarters, deep in a game of chess. Emily was too restive to read, and she didn't dare take a walk in the moonlight. Not while Lyon Gallant was on the island, though Ivy had said he was entertaining. The housekeeper would never breach her employer's privacy, but Emily had a feeling "entertaining" meant he was with a woman.

She experienced an odd twinge about that, and couldn't fathom why. She disliked the man intensely. His playboy life-style was none of her concern.

Turning her mind to calmer, happier thoughts, she decided, since Mr. Gallant was "entertaining," it was safe to wander onto the patio. His private wing was on the far side of the house with its own courtyard. There would be little danger of running into him.

After the party last night, brightly upholstered wicker furniture had been returned to the patio, but Emily didn't feel like sitting.

She ambled to the railing, inhaling the sea-laden air and the sweetness of a tropical night. She found herself smiling. What a lovely place Sin Island was. It should be called Heaven Island or Little Eden or... Her musings faded and she frowned, listening. Was that whistling? Yes. She could hear someone whistling a tune off in the distance. She recognized the song as the same one she and her irritating host had danced to last night.

She could also detect the sound of approaching footsteps. With foreboding building in her chest, she turned. The foreboding blossomed into full-blown panic. It was Lyon Gallant! He was strolling toward her, backlit by the light from the patio doors. He was wearing a white knit shirt and white slacks, and the golden aura highlighted his wide shoulders and trim hips. His face was in shadow, but the whistling suggested he was in a good mood. She couldn't say the same about herself.

Not anymore.

''Evening, Miss Stone.'' He came up beside her and leaned one of those trim hips on the metal railing. ''How was that?''

She wanted to cry, to scream, but she forced herself to remain poised, remarking flippantly, "You lounge against the railing like a professional lounger. Congratulations."

He chuckled. "No, I meant, the whistling. I didn't want you to think I was jumping out at you in the dark again."

She stiffened, abashed by the reminder. "How kind."

"Now, why don't we get started." He placed a hand on the rail, leaning slightly toward her. "Tell me what you need to know most urgently."

Her breath quickened and she grew hot all over. "Haven't you teased me enough about the sex lessons?" she cried. "I've put it completely from my mind, and if you were truly a gentleman, you would, too!"

There was a spark of something indefinable in his eyes. If she was to have guessed, she would have thought it surprise. But it was quickly gone, replaced by mild amusement. "I was referring to your project."

"I know! You're forever harping on that! I wish I'd never—" She stopped herself, some small part of her mind suggesting she delay her rantings for a minute and ask one important question. "Project?" It came out sheepish.

He nodded as a cool breeze swept across the patio, ruffling his hair. "The west wing?" he prodded with a half-grin. It was obvious he was trying to remain all business, but her outraged protest was making it hard for him. "Your associate, Mrs. Dillburg, said you had to speak with me—most urgently—on some matter about the redecorating project."

Meg! This was all Meg's doing! She vowed to strangle her friend at the first possible opportunity. What was she going to say now? She didn't know anything at all about the project.

"Oh, I—I'm sorry." Her mind flew in all directions to find a way out of this predicament. "It's just that, er..." Her memory caught on something she'd read in a magazine a few days ago while she was lounging by the pool, about a new designer's work. She hadn't liked the man's designs, probably the reason she recalled the story so vividly. She prayed Lyon Gallant wouldn't, either. "I just—just wanted to make sure about one of the second-floor rooms. Um—my computer printout says you specified a gilded Bohemian style day bed with golden swags and tassels and—and black flocked wallpaper?''

His brows knit in wry amusement. ''Sounds like I'm opening a brothel.''

She swallowed. So far, so good. ''That— that's why I'm asking. You know about our computer foul-up. Well, considering your— your classic taste, it didn't quite sound like you.''

''I'm gratified.'' He inclined his head, his expression going from wry to skeptical. ''Why are we really here?''

''I don't know what you mean.'' She'd done the best she could. Those few words were the extent of her interior designer terminology. If he wasn't buying that, she was dead.

''I mean, I've never known the design firm you work for to make such a serious error.'' The patio was dark except for a pale spill of light from the French doors and the dastardly moon. Shadows from the palmettos danced fitfully across his rugged features, but even so, she could see high suspicion in his gaze. She ran her hands down her cotton skirt, smoothing it, fidgeting, wondering what was running through his mind. "What do you want, sweetheart?" he asked almost gently. "Another kiss?"

A flush burned her face. She'd assumed he was starting to realize she was a fraud. She'd had no idea he was still thinking such a crazy thing—though, in the strictest sense, he might be right. "Certainly not!" she objected breathlessly. Even to her own ears, she didn't sound convincing.

His gaze sparked with new intent, frightening her. "Your instincts were good. Calling me out here on such a flimsy pretense. I didn't know you had that much subterfuge in you." He moved in front of her, adding, "Bold but ladylike."

"I'm *not*!" she objected, so rattled she wasn't sure which argument she'd meant to present.

"Which?" He curled his fingers around the railing on either side of her.

Trapped! Gloriously trapped! Some traitorous part of her brain was rejoicing, but most of her was trembling with protest. In her heart, she knew if she struggled he'd let her walk away. But she couldn't conjure up any desire to leave, not even if her life depended on it. Snared by her own weakness, she stood before him, defeated yet full of anticipation. "What?" She breathed the word, not sure what they were talking about anymore.

He grinned, and with slow, dangerous premeditation, leaned toward her. "It's time for lesson two, sweetheart." His breath was heated and welcome against her lips. "First, lift your chin a little."

With a shaky sigh, she complied, wondering at herself. It seemed as though she was looking on helplessly as her body stripped itself of every shred of moral fiber. His powerful forearms grazed hers. So warm, so solid. She didn't want to look into his eyes, but she couldn't help herself. She was afraid he would see into her mind, sense her hesitation, her fear, and worse, her longing...

"Good. Now lean slightly away, but give me a coy smile."

She had no trouble with the leaning away part, but the smile was more difficult. Clearly the lucid fragment that was left of her brain still controlled her lips, and they refused to flirt.

"Try, sweetheart," he coaxed, his voice low, disarming. "A man needs a little encouragement."

"I—I don't do coy." She was startled to hear her voice, but even more startled by what she'd admitted. She couldn't intend to actually go through with this—this lesson, could she?

"Then try thinking about kneeing me in the groin," he suggested.

Her lips twitched upward.

"Perfect." White teeth glinted, destroying her already tattered defenses. "Now, pretend I'm Brad Pitt."

"Who?"

Any interest in who Brad Pitt might be was swept away as his lips took possession of hers, sending wild shivers of pleasure through her body. His mouth was hot, yet gentle, as his lips caressed hers. The tender hunger of his kiss found some long-hidden emptiness inside her and began to fill it up. She pressed against him, his taut, hard skin burning her where she touched, then clutched.

His hands moved from the railing to enfold her, to pull her against him, allowing her no shyness as he massaged, stimulated. She was surprised to find that her hands were moving, too, seeming to know on their own what to do. His back was broad, and its muscled texture excited her fingertips as she explored, learned, craved to know more.

"Lyon?" A far-off female voice intruded into Emily's brain. She heard his low moan and realized the kiss she was reveling in was ending. Slowly, he drew his mouth from hers. "You learn fast," he said, his voice only a breath of sound. "Lesson three will require fewer clothes." Startling her, he grazed her earlobe with his teeth before backing away. "But for now, I'm afraid I've been neglecting my guest."

"Lyon?" The voice was closer, just inside the French doors.

He stepped away and turned, his smile polite, as though he'd just been complimenting her on her exquisite taste in flocked wallpaper. "Out here, Athena," he called, the huskiness barely detectable in his voice.

Unstrung, she sagged against the rail, assailed by a sense of loss. Her throat ached as she worked to swallow a sob. She felt so cheap. So easy! This wasn't like her at all!

He had moved aside, and she could see the open double doors as a woman emerged. Even in her gloom, Emily's lips opened in awe. Lyon's female guest was over six feet tall, with graceful, elongated limbs, reminiscent of the expensive Italian porcelains by Lladro. Her hair was platinum and cut boyishly short over most of her head, with wisps combed toward her face. At her nape, long, silky locks caught the breeze and made her look ethereal, like an angel with a bent for basketball.

The woman came to Lyon on a cloud of airy fabric that must have been a swimsuit cover-up. For Emily could see a two-piece white bathing suit underneath the flowing, sheer fabric. At least that's what she hoped it was.

The blonde's lips were pouty and full, enhanced by an attractive overbite. Her cheekbones were lethal. Her lids lolled torpidly over half-closed eyes, and her lashes were too long to be real. "Lyon," she called again, her voice

high-pitched and grating. "I decided I wanted
to swim in the ocean." She floated up beside
him. In four-inch wedge sandals, she was not
quite his height. Probably a nice change for
a woman who towered over most people—
man or woman. "Come with me?" She entwined her fingers in his, and Emily had a
feeling the action was a perfect example of
coy.

"I'm not wearing a swimsuit." His grin was
easy.

She laughed, an unattractive sound. "Oh,
Lyon. You're so funny."

He faced Emily. "Miss Stone. This is my
guest, Athena. Perhaps you know of her?"

Emily was at a loss. "If she's a Greek
goddess, I do." Looking at the lovely woman,
the possibility didn't seem like much of a
stretch, if pure, physical beauty was any
yardstick.

Athena made that screeching sound again
that passed for laughter.

"She's a model," Lyon explained. "Some
would say a supermodel."

"Some?" Athena pretended displeasure. "And I thought you really wanted me in your catalogue, Lyon."

He smiled. "Athena, this is Miss Stone, my interior designer."

Athena's smile faded. "No kidding?" She gave Emily her first direct look, her lazy lids coming up in surprise. "You dress more like a linoleum saleslady."

Emily couldn't respond, not sure if she'd been insulted.

"Miss Stone?" Lyon's tone was vaguely irritated as he drew her gaze. "I'm sure Athena meant that nicely. You see, she used to sell linoleum."

"Don't remind me!" The model laughed that abrasive laugh, then seemed to get Lyon's mild reprimand, and her smile dimmed. "Oh, sorry. I didn't mean it as a slam. You just dress sorta frumpy for a designer. No offense?"

"How could she take offense?" Lyon chided softly, but the rebuff seemed to go over the thin woman's head. Instead of looking chagrined, she leaned flirtatiously toward

Lyon. "What about that swim? Then we can get back to negotiating my contract."

His smile was charming, and Emily hated the affect it had on her, even though it wasn't directed her way. "I'll play lifeguard," he assured the model.

She giggled, flapping her lashes. "I have to warn you. I'm a *bad* swimmer!"

He nodded toward Emily. "Good night, Miss Stone."

She tried her voice, but it had vanished. She could only nod. After the couple left, she absently licked her lips. She realized she still tasted of him, and her heart constricted. *Cavalier* had been too kind a word for the way this man treated lovemaking.

She glared at the moon with stinging, reproachful eyes. "You should be ashamed!" Even as she said it, she knew she was talking more to herself than to the glowing slice of moon. It was her fault if she felt despondent. She'd just stood there like a fool and *let* him kiss her, knowing the way he affected her.

It wasn't all her fault, she realized. Not entirely. And it wasn't all Lyon Gallant's fault, either. He was merely doing what came naturally to a libidinous playboy.

She heard Athena's grating laugh in the distance and closed her eyes, utterly miserable. The last thing she needed was to witness Lyon Gallant and Athena "negotiating" on the beach.

Balling her fists, she stalked toward the French doors, plotting Meg's murder.

CHAPTER FIVE

"I'M NOT speaking to you," Meg pouted as she flounced into Emily's room.

Slipping on her terry swimsuit cover-up, Emily turned toward her friend, confused. "What have I done?"

"You're mad at me, and I don't speak to people who are mad at me."

"That's probably a good plan." Emily smiled. It was hard to stay angry with Meg, and she'd gotten over being upset hours ago. "But we spent the day in Miami while Ivy did the weekly shopping, and you talked to me the entire time. I can't see why you've taken on this policy of silence now." She cinched up her short robe. "Especially since I got my hair cut and permed the way you insisted, and I bought this sapphire tank suit that matches my eyes simply so you wouldn't have a fit in the store."

"I don't care! I still say—oh, before I forget..." Meg fished in her lacy cover-up pocket and held out a plastic bag. "Here's the peas you wanted for the fish." She scanned her friend with squinty concentration. "As I was saying, with your hair soft and curly around your face like that, it makes your eyes seem huge. Admit it, Emily. The haircut is perfect for you. And that swimsuit—though it's a little conservative for my tastes—is lovely with your coloring."

Emily stuck the bag of peas in her pocket, surveying herself critically. The shorter bob did give her a softer, more feminine look, she supposed. And being a practical person, she decided it was a good length for summertime. As for the suit, it fit, and she'd needed a new one, anyway.

"But what good is it all?" Meg's pretty face puckered as she plopped down on the four-poster bed. "Even when I throw you into Mr. Gallant's arms, you refuse his every overture!"

Emily flushed. She hadn't been one hundred percent successful at *that*, so far, but decided not to mention last night's kiss. "Meg, I told you. He was with a woman. A beautiful model. It was humiliating."

"Okay." Meg frowned as though in thought—not a good sign. Crossing her legs, she toyed with the tie on her cover-up. "I believe I've come up with a foolproof backup plan."

Emily shook her head, unused to the feel of delicate curls nudging her forehead and cheeks. "I don't want to hear it. If you want to go swimming, let's go. We only have an hour or so of sunlight left."

"In the cove."

Emily had grabbed her snorkel and mask but came to an abrupt halt. "Where?"

Meg bounced up. "The cove." She shrugged. "If you don't like Mr. Gallant, then there's always Mr. Sexy Handyman."

Emily's lips dropped open. She'd never *told* Meg! Clamping her jaws tight, she shook her head. "Oh, dear," she moaned. "Come on, Meg. It's a long, embarrassing story."

By the time they got to the beach Meg was laughing so hard she had to wipe away tears. "And you told the carpenter you were having an affair with Mr. Gallant, and he *was* Mr. Gallant?" She unfurled her beach towel. "Emily Stone! And I thought *I* did nutty stuff! No wonder you don't want to have anything to do with him. He sure played you for a dope.''

Emily felt a shudder of renewed humiliation. ''You put things so delicately, you should be in the diplomatic service.''

''I know. We'd be at war all the time.'' Meg guffawed, dropping to her towel. ''But that's why quiet types like you and Larry love me. I'm uncomplicated and spontaneous. Not like you deep thinkers.'' She shrugged off her cover-up. ''Well, all this laughing has tired me out. You go feed fish. I'm going to take a nap and catch some rays. But don't worry, I'll come up with something.''

''Just sleep, don't *think*!'' Emily warned, taking off her cover-up and laying it beside the beach towel.

Meg flopped to her stomach, then peered at her friend, giggling and shaking her head incredulously before she closed her eyes.

''You're a real comfort,'' Emily muttered, but found her lips quirking upward as she entered the lapping tidewater. For all Meg's nosiness and meddling, she managed to lift Emily's spirits when they most needed lifting.

And wasn't that what friendship was all about?

Though she didn't swim well, there wasn't much swimming talent required in snorkeling. In shallow water, she squatted to put her mask below the surface and breathed through her snorkel, scattering peas in the tide to attract colorful fish. As she moved into deeper water, she began to float on her stomach. She'd always been a good floater.

The fish were like an undulating rainbow in the shallow sea as they vied for peas. The most bold ones even nudged her arms and legs as they swarmed by, making her giggle.

Time flew. When the sunset lit the sky with violet flame, she stood and stretched, out of peas and almost out of visibility. Even though the water was clear, it was getting too dark to see under the surface. She turned to walk toward the shore and was horrified by what she saw.

Instead of Meg sound asleep on a beach towel, Lyon Gallant was standing thigh deep in sloshing surf, grinning at her. The only good thing about the picture was—he wasn't naked.

"Small world." He moved her way.

The warm evening breeze ruffled her hair, making wet curls dance before her eyes. Nervously, she brushed them back. "A little *too* small," she muttered.

He shrugged nonchalantly, muscles rippling with the action. "It is my island. You shouldn't be too shocked if you run into me."

"I didn't for the first two weeks!"

His grin broadened. "Yes, you did."

She blanched. He was right, of course. "But—but I didn't know who you were."

"True."

Embarrassed by the reminder, she sloshed past him, avoiding eye contact. "Well—I don't want to keep you."

"I like your hair short."

Startled, she flicked a glance his way.

"And the suit's nice, too."

He towered there with one taut hip cocked, his lazy gaze quickening her pulse. The sunset was blindingly beautiful behind him, coloring the quiet sea scarlet. He stood before her, so still, glistening with sea spray, he looked like Poseidon, just risen from the ocean depths. Burnished light spilled over him with the same fluid power as the Atlantic, throwing the muscles of his arms and shoulders into sharp relief.

He was the image of a pagan god. It was no wonder he refused to have his picture taken. His island paradise would be forever besieged by wild-eyed, screaming women. They would invade day and night, in all manner of floating craft, if they knew such masculine perfection was secreted only a few miles south of Miami's beaches.

Feeling awkward, she shifted her mask and snorkel from one hand to the other. "Um, thanks—about my hair and—whatever..." Not knowing what more to do, she spun away, tromping toward dry land.

Her shadow was drawn out and slanted along the wet sand in front of her. In a moment his shadow loomed large beside hers. "Remember what I said last night?"

She didn't look at him, but shook her head. He'd said a lot of things, things engraved on her brain, but she didn't plan to admit it.

"About lesson three?"

She swallowed hard, trying to form a non-answer. "I—I have to find Meg."

"Mrs. Dillburg has gone back to the house."

Emily bit her lip.

"She told me to tell you." There was vague humor in his tone. "Miss Stone, you're avoiding the subject."

"I refuse to discuss that with you. Go *away*!"

His shadow disobeyed, continuing to accompany hers. "Why? Have you found somebody else to teach you about hot sex?"

Shocked by his bluntness, she turned on him. "I'm not having hot sex with anybody!"

"Oh?" He inclined his head, mischief in his eyes. "I thought, since you weren't jogging through the cove anymore, you'd found a sex teacher you prefer over me."

Refusing to be goaded, she set her fists on her hips. "Of course I haven't!"

His rich chuckle grated on her nerves.

"I'm thrilled you find my lack of sex appeal so hilarious!" She turned on her heel to escape.

"Not at all. I'm brokenhearted."

"I can tell."

He took her hand in his, and the small act of possession was galvanizing. He couldn't have halted her more thoroughly if she'd been bound and gagged. "Sweetheart," he said, coming up to face her. "No woman lacks sex appeal when handled right." He touched her chin with a coaxing finger, prodding her to look at him. "Let me prove it to you."

His midnight gaze clung to hers, making promises so eloquent she ached for the fulfillment he silently pledged.

That assurance in his eyes affected her like nothing in her life had ever done before. She could feel herself melting, sinking, losing her resolve. Even as she shook her head in denial, her arms rose on their own to encircle his neck, fondling the velvety hair at his nape. "This isn't right," she breathed.

"It's perfect." He lifted her into his arms, and the thrill of it swept away her intended redress—that she'd been faulting their actions, not questioning her technique.

As if by sorcery, she found herself on a blanket. His kisses began as gentle and undemanding as the warm breeze that caressed them, and she responded eagerly, kissing him back, savoring every lingering moment.

He whispered encouragement, suggestions. The approval he offered when she responded kindled fledgling feelings of competence within her. She emulated his love play, and with each tender reassurance, she grew stronger, more capable. She even began to allow herself to react on instinct, surprised and pleased when her tentative efforts elicited his praise.

So pure and sensuous was Lyon's coaching she soon didn't recognize herself under his expertise. The schoolteacher was certainly being taught the finer points of seduction. The hands, the lips, the tongue, the teeth, all had special, pleasing tasks to perform. And Lyon Gallant knew each and every one to perfection.

His knowing hand searched a path down her side, along her thigh, the easy massage sending currents of desire through her as the sweetness of his kisses grew deeper, more demanding. He slid atop her, and the feel of his skin against hers was exhilarating, making the blood pound in her brain and leap in her heart.

His kisses moved downward, warm and sweet, to tantalize her throat, her shoulder, nipping, exciting. She mirrored his actions, stroking, tasting. She was becoming a different Emily from the one she'd known an hour ago. A *feeling* Emily—for the first time in her life—and she rejoiced in her burgeoning wisdom.

Except for their swimsuits, they were body to body, man touching woman. His lips reached the edge of her suit and a groan from deep in his throat startled her. She had no idea he was feeling the same wild desire as she, and that stilled her heart. She caressed the length of his hard back, loving the rigid yet supple feel of him against her tingling palms.

He slipped a finger beneath the strap of her suit, dragging it off her shoulder, then kissing the spot where it had been. Sliding his hand down, he brushed the rise of her breast, murmuring huskily, "It's time for lesson four, sweetheart."

One questing finger dipped below the confines of her suit, making shocking contact with softer flesh, and she gasped with the un-accustomed touch. Her body cried out that he go on, hold her intimately, make full and complete love to her, but her mind pleaded desperately for reason. *Emily, just last night he was with another woman!* The reminder was cruel torture for her, and she whimpered.

The frightened, frail sound brought his head up, his eyes clouding with disbelief.

''Please,'' she cried. ''I can't do this.''

He stared at her, his brows dipping. He seemed almost disconcerted. ''Don't say that, sweetheart.'' His voice was rough with passion, and she could tell he was having a hard time with her decision to back off this late in the deed.

She was so shaky, her bones so insub-stantial, she couldn't push him away. She had to rely on his honor—*pray* that he was hon-orable. ''I—I'm sorry. I know it's hard for a man to stop...''

His jaw worked for a long minute, but he didn't speak. Emily had no strength to do anything but stare into his hawkish face as the last, pink remnants of the sunset tinted his features, highlighting a smoldering inner fire in his eyes.

Or was it merely the sunset that burned in his gaze? Frowning, she searched the dark depths, watched them spark with exasperation and something else. Some secret struggle. Was it frustration? Probably. She knew he was upset. What man wouldn't be? But he said nothing. Didn't try to intimidate or cajole.

After a strained silence, she was amazed to see a rueful smile edge onto his lips. ''If you want me to admire your morals, Miss Stone, give me time.'' With that, he rolled off her and stood. She was further startled when he offered her a hand.

Wordlessly, still in an odd state of shock, she accepted, and he tugged her to her feet. She swayed unsteadily, but decided she had bones after all, and could support herself, though she wasn't as stable as she'd like to be.

While she stood there feeling dizzy, Lyon shook out the blanket and folded it. Once it was under his arm, he nudged her. ''You okay?''

She came out of her stupor and nodded, taking a step away. He took her arm, pulling her back. "Wrong way, Columbus."

She couldn't help but peer at his face. He flashed a cavalier grin. She was upset not only by the way that grin made her tremble, but by the fact that he could so quickly put aside what had almost happened between them. He indicated the other direction. "Try this way."

"My cover up..." She found it peculiar that her mind would leap to such an unimportant subject.

"We'll pass by it."

She scowled at him, confused. "Why are you being nice to me? I thought you'd be mad."

It was dark now but for the rising moon, and when he turned away toward the sea, she couldn't guess his expression. For a second, she thought she saw his square jaw clench. "You catch more flies with honey, sweetheart. If I'm nice, you might change your mind about lesson four." Checking the luminous dial of his watch, he added, "Right now, I have to get back for a late meeting in

Miami." He looked at her. "Do you know where you're going?"

A sudden, unreasoning fury choked her. How dare he be so casual about what almost happened! Maybe it was merely another tumble in the sand to him, but to her, it had been . . .

She didn't want to think about what it had been. But she had a feeling she would never be quite the same after tonight. "I know exactly where I'm going, Mr. Gallant! And it's away from you!"

His brows lifted in surprise, which upset her even more. Was he so much the unfeeling lecher he couldn't conceive of why she was hurt? "One more thing!" she blurted. "Don't—don't come near me with that— that..." She poked a finger toward his mouth, unable to say the word, for her lips still tingled from his mind-altering kisses. "Or—or those—those..." She gestured broadly at his shoulders. "Is—is that—am I making myself—" Her voice broke. Too upset to speak, she glared at him.

There was hesitation in his eyes as he watched her, clearly baffled.

Frustrated beyond words at his lack of penitence, she stalked away from him, feeling stupidly forsaken. It had been such a wrong, *dumb* fantasy to want to have a fling with Lyon Gallant. Even though she'd stopped herself before things went too far, she knew the encounter would take its toll. She was afraid that, for her, at least, it had been a life-changing experience, and her heart lurched with regret.

How could he be so nonchalant about it? The answer was painfully obvious by the puzzlement in his expression. Lyon Gallant had escapades like this every day of the week. They were never important to him—and probably never cut short by a panicky virgin, either. He must think of her as a silly child.

She broke into a run to further distance herself from him. With tears streaming down her cheeks, she faced the awful fact that she was falling for a man who was sexually accessible, yet emotionally, utterly inaccessible.

How could a sensible biology teacher be turned into a blubbering half-wit by a playboy with nothing more substantial on his agenda than a few sex lessons?

* * *

Emily was reading by the pool when she heard the big helicopter approaching. Ivy came rushing outside, looking uncharacteristically flushed. "My dear." She motioned frantically. "I'm afraid Mr. Gallant has come back today specifically to speak with you and Meg."

Emily jumped up from the lounge chair, her magazine dropping to the tile deck. "To see Meg and me?" she echoed, fright slithering through her. "Why?"

Ivy shook her head, obviously distressed. "About the west wing." Her tone was dejected. "I have no idea why he's suddenly developed a personal interest, but..."

Emily was already dashing past Ivy. "I'll change and get in there. Where's Meg?"

"Panicking."

"Tell her I'll meet her in the west wing."

"Oh dear," was all Emily heard.

Her heart thudding, she swiftly changed into a summer dress and sandals and grabbed her notebook and a ruler, since she couldn't find her tape measure. She hoped Meg had one, for she didn't think many interior designers measured with a twelve-inch stick.

When she reached the west wing, Meg was waving for her to hurry. She was wearing a minidress of red knit. Emily decided it probably looked more like what an interior designer might wear than her knee-length empire-style dress. More important, her friend was carrying a tape measure.

Once inside the nearest room, Meg indicated a stack of fabric and wallpaper books. "You pretend to be going over this stuff. I'll shout out measurements."

Emily nodded, hating herself but fearful for Ivy's job. She dropped to her knees and picked a book at random while Meg flew to the nearest window. "Okay," she called. "I'm measuring."

Emily swallowed, her heart pounding as Meg went to work.

"Write down seventy-four inches by thirty-three inches," she called after a few awkward minutes while she figured out how to work the tape.

Emily flipped open her notebook, then grimaced. "I don't have a pencil!"

"Will this do?" came a deep voice at her back. Her heart dropped. How had he sneaked up on them so silently? Apparently he could do it even without moonlight.

Trying to appear nonchalant, she turned and forced a smile. "Oh, Mr. Gallant." He was holding out a gold pen. "Oh—thank you." Taking it, she mumbled, "I—I must have dropped mine somewhere." Since the room was bare, it was a feeble excuse. Even a pencil would be visible in the vast, empty chamber.

Feeling a blush creep up her cheeks, she turned back and drew a blank. "What were those dimensions?"

Meg's eyes went wide, and it was clear she'd blurted out the numbers and didn't remember them. "Uh—"

"Seventy-four by thirty-three," Lyon helped.

Emily grimaced, but since her back was to him, he wouldn't know. "Um, thanks." She scribbled.

"And what was the fabric for those drapes?"

Emily felt sick. She gave Meg a helpless look but Meg had ambled to the next window, pretending to measure it, though it looked exactly the same size as the other five along that wall. With a despondent exhale, she jabbed at a book. "It's in here." She started thumbing through, then belatedly realized she'd pointed out a wallpaper book. *Oh, lord!*

He knelt beside her. "Daring concept, using wallpaper for window draperies."

She shrugged, trying to smile. "Oh, this book looks so much like the—the other one."

"Ah." He nodded, his gaze nailing hers. She saw skepticism glittering there, though neither his tone or his expression gave it away—yet.

"This window's the same," Meg reported.

"What a surprise." This time Lyon allowed a tinge of sarcasm into his words.

Emily felt like a criminal as she scribbled, "The same on window two."

"What about that fabric?" Lyon prodded.

Emily eyed the books. One had the word *fabric* on the cover, so she grabbed it. "This is the book I meant to get."

"Yes. This green one is a dead ringer for that pink one," he said.

She cast a nervous gaze his way, but tried to pretend he hadn't spoken. "Well, let's see now—"

"Miss Stone," he interrupted as she nervously thumbed through the book with absolutely no idea what to do next.

"Yes?" she asked, deciding one damask, off-white material seemed quite nice. She wasn't sure how much original input he'd had on the decorating. If he knew very much, he'd know this was wrong. If he didn't, she'd be safe and so would Ivy's job. But she wasn't a risk-taker, and even lying about a relatively nondescript square of cloth was more of a gamble than she was comfortable taking. "This is nice," she tried lamely.

"Yes."

She chewed on the inside of her cheek. His monosyllabic answer hadn't been much help, and neither was his nearness. He seemed to loom almost all around her.

"Window three is the same," Meg chirped, apparently having a wonderful time, not even noticing the grilling Emily was being put through.

Fumbling again for her notebook, she wrote falteringly, "Window three, same." Lyon's after-shave was invading her senses, and it was hard for her to deal with his ominous closeness. He'd laid a hand on the page to help keep it down, brushing her fingers with his. Though she'd quickly shifted away, she experienced his touch all the way to her chest, where she felt a heaviness that made her breathing difficult. "Are you sure this is right, Miss Stone?" he queried near her ear.

She swallowed. Agitated, she cast a glance at Meg, who'd moved on to window four. Emily was afraid if she sang out "The same," one more time, she'd start giggling from pure hysteria. Pulling herself together, she offered, "Well, I—I could check my printout."

"I thought you said your computer fouled up. What good would that do?"

He had made a troubling point. "I mean— I believe this is the one Ivy decided on. I'll just go check my notes." She struggled to her feet, intent on making an escape, but he was faster, standing and blocking the exit.

"Window four, the same," Meg announced with a smile.

Both Emily and Lyon turned to face her. Emily couldn't keep from shooting her friend a help-me look. Meg's triumphant smile faded. ''Something wrong?''

''I'm going to borrow your partner for a minute.'' He took Emily's elbow. ''I'd appreciate her expert advice about something in my suite.''

''Do you need me?'' Meg called, and Emily was sure her friend was dying to see Lyon's private quarters.

''You're too indispensable here,'' Lyon said without turning back.

Emily was herded down hallways she'd never seen before and never even wanted to know existed. Lyon's hand at her elbow was insistent, though painless. She clutched her notepad and his pen for dear life, praying she could get through whatever this was without giving away their lie. She also found herself issuing up a new prayer—pleading that he didn't intend to ravish her in the privacy of his quarters, calling it lesson four. Well, she didn't actually think it would be a ravishment. All he had to do was grin that irresistible grin and kiss her a time or two.

She was only half resisting when they got to a foyer with a black marble floor and white marble walls. Even as stark as the vestibule was, it seemed strong and tasteful, making a statement about its occupant.

Beside a set of white enameled doors, ten feet tall, stood a towering bronze statue of a Pompeian wrestler. It was striking in the sparse, contemporary setting. A skylight illuminated a lush tropical plant that spread its fronds in welcome before the shiny marble wall on the opposite side of the doors. She knew at once this was the entrance to Lyon's private lair.

When he led her through the doors, her senses reeled with the stark elegance of the place. Dramatic lighting seemed to ooze from the very walls. And everything she saw screamed money and taste.

Her stomach knotted. She was so far out of her element, she wanted to die. But he led her on, through the living room that emphasized a Roman marble torso and a white leather seating area, before smoked glass doors that led onto a courtyard that looked like a piece of Eden.

Artwork was strategically placed on the white marble walls, all bold lines and geometric shapes. But Emily noticed there were no faces in the pictures, no photographs, either. She shivered inwardly. No matter how exquisite the place was, it seemed cold and somehow lonely.

Her mind blurred and stumbled. What in heaven's name was she thinking? This suite probably cost a million all by itself, and the brightest, most sought-after designers had used all their talents to make it what it was. How dare she have the nerve to think of it as cold and lonely. What was she even doing here? It was painfully clear she could never fool this man into thinking she knew anything about decorating.

They went through another door, and her heart tripped and faltered. She knew which room this was. Just as in the other rooms, understatement and studied elegance characterized Lyon's bedroom. It was immense, and also sparsely furnished, one wall filled with arched window groupings. There were three windows to a group. Outside she could see his private pool and more enchanting landscaping. About six feet in from the wall, in front of the outer two window groupings, stood white stone columns. The floor was the same black marble as everywhere in his suite, its white and silver veining giving the surface a deep, liquid look.

Between the columns, almost in the center of the room, lounged a huge bed set in a heavy, white enameled frame, the bedspread made of a shimmering white fabric. The thing seemed to float there on a field of indirect lighting. Emily was amazed at the mysterious sensation it gave her—as though she'd entered an exotic world that celebrated pleasures of the flesh. She was sure her expression showed her fearful awe.

The only blot on the erotic magnificence of the place was an undulating blue smudge on one marble wall. Every so often the smudge seemed to depict bits and pieces of female anatomy, and she blanched to realize a buxom, nude woman had rolled along the surface to make that lewd blemish.

"What do you think?" he asked.

She jumped, though he'd spoken softly, and her glance swept the grand room again.

"I—I think it's all so—so unreal," she breathed. "I've never seen a bedroom like this. It's like sleeping on a stage or in outer space."

He chuckled. "I meant the blue paint on the marble."

Her glance slid to the pornographic smudge, and she frowned. "That's awful. What are you going to do about it?" She looked at him, concerned.

He laughed, a deep, rich celebration, its echo warming and humanizing the vast space. "I thought I was asking you that question, Miss Stone. You *are* the decorator." He paused and a brow rose almost as though in challenge. "Aren't you?"

CHAPTER SIX

EMILY was shaken by his low question and guarded scrutiny, but forced herself to remember Ivy's predicament. The housekeeper had taken a great chance in letting Meg and her come here under this guise. Even though she hadn't known about the ruse until it was too late, that didn't absolve her of the responsibility if Ivy lost her job. Clutching her notebook, she cleared her throat, taking pains to look like a professional.

Dodging Lyon Gallant's gaze, she marched over to the wall and gave it a close inspection, trying to think what an interior designer might suggest. New marble came to mind, since the paint had webbed outward from the larger stain, making tiny blue streaks in the natural veins. The paint was so deeply insinuated into the wall it didn't look like any cleaner could get it out without ruining the marble completely.

She shrugged. "It's pretty bad, isn't it?"

He made no comment, but she could hear the click of his heels as he drew near.

She put a fingernail against the paint and scratched lightly. "Why did your—guest—do this?" She bit the inside of her cheek. That was none of her business, for heaven's sake!

"I have no idea," he said, sounding as though he meant it.

She couldn't help but turn and look at him. He was staring at the paint, too, appearing puzzled. It was the same expression he'd exhibited on the beach when she'd been angry at him, angry that he hadn't realized he'd hurt her or didn't care that he had. The memory brought back her feelings of regret and dejection, and she shook her head in sorrow. "Maybe it was her way of trying to leave a mark on your life."

He gave her a sideways glance, looking broadsided. "What?"

She flinched at his malevolent tone, but was so upset she ignored it and flung a hand toward the blue stain. "Do you really *not* know why women get upset with you, or is it that you don't care?"

He didn't respond, but his brows knit and his stare hardened.

Apparently a man like Lyon Gallant, with such dynamic drive and shrewd business genius, found it difficult to believe that another person's attitude might differ radically from his own, that a woman could be mad at him, frustrated by his lack of commitment. "Did you tell her you appreciated the use of her body but you had a meeting in Miami and maybe you'd see her again sometime?"

Anger flickered to life in the midnight of his eyes. "Since you've made it clear you don't want to be a part of my sex life, Miss Stone, I don't see what business it is of yours." His tone, though quiet, held an ominous quality. "Now, about my wall?" He arched an intimidating brow, effectively closing the discussion of his life-style.

She burned with resentment and knew she must be a bright crimson. But she was no fool. She didn't intend to argue with him, not about something she didn't even want to think about.

The smart course would be to get this over as quickly as possible. She had to try to carry on the sham, then get out of there without revealing the lie. Stiffly she faced the vandalism, inhaling to maintain control. She was no designer, but she wasn't an imbecile. Surely she could make a sensible suggestion that wouldn't give her away as a fraud. "Well," she croaked, then cleared the anxiety from her voice. "You could move a dresser in front of it."

He was silent.

"Or—or a big plant."

More silence.

"Or both." Unable to stand the extended quiet, she chanced a look at him. His brows were still knit, but his expression was more incredulous than angry. *Oh, dear, he hated the idea.* A dresser! What had she been thinking? There was probably a huge closet somewhere nearby with enough built-in drawers to accommodate a small country.

Well, darn him, she didn't care anymore, and her damaged pride compelled her to say so. "To be honest, Mr. Gallant, this room is so flawless it should be on the cover of every design magazine in the world. It would make an outstanding bank lobby. But it's *not* a bank; it's your home. You should add natural woods to warm the place. Maybe some flowers. Roses are especially nice. My mother raised them and I took over her gardens after she died. When they're in season, I always have bouquets in my house. They smell wonderful and they cheer a room.''

She swept her hand around. "This is a cold place, Mr. Gallant. There's nothing warm and alive in here." His nostrils flared, and she realized she'd insulted him. *He* lived here, after all. "I'm sorry," she mumbled, a little repentant that she'd allowed her hurt pride such free reign. But he always seemed to prick her just enough to drive her over the edge of tact. "Well . . ." She grimaced, knowing she couldn't call back her words. "That's the way I feel."

His jaws tight, he leaned against the smudge and cast his gaze to the wall of windows. His features carried little information as he stared into space, and she wondered what he was thinking. Surely her opinion didn't matter to him.

After a moment he chuckled morosely, his glance flicking to her face. "A dresser and a big plant?" His smile was more wry than amused. "That's extremely practical for an interior designer, Miss Stone. I would have thought you'd suggest I have it commercially polished, or remarbled."

She felt deflated and leaned against the wall, registering its innate chill. It was growing depressingly clear that he knew more about the subject than she did. "Of course," she muttered, wishing she was dead, "that's another obvious option."

"I could burn it down, too."

She jerked to look at him in time to see a flash of teeth. "It would be warmer—at least for awhile."

He was *teasing* her! Affronted, she straightened. "If you're through with me, I'll go back to help Meg."

"Help her do what?" He stood away from the wall, his lips twitching into a determined line. "Your charade has gone on long enough. It's time you told me what you're really doing on my island." She stared in shock as he raked her with a severe glance. "Well?"

Pure, black terror spiraled through her. Oh, *no*! It was the stupid dresser idea that had given her away, she was sure. Why couldn't she have kept her pride out of it and just said he'd have to replace the marble?

"Oh, please," she begged in a sickly whisper, touching his arm, then quickly re-thinking that idea. It wasn't wise to touch this man. "Please, whatever you do, don't fire Ivy. She was just being kind," she confessed unhappily. "It's my fault. All my fault!" Her voice broke, and she began to shake with re-action, because he'd discovered the lie and because dark foreboding hovered in his eyes. Clutching her fists together, she made herself stare into his damning gaze, imploring silently.

"Ivy?" He sounded more startled than angry that someone he trusted would con-spire against him.

"She was trying to help me heal after Harry left me at the——" She caught herself, pulling her lips between her teeth. The last thing she wanted was to dredge up the fact that she was a total washout at holding onto her own fiancé. It was bad enough to have to talk about it at all, but worse—much worse—to have to admit it to this man, of all the people in the world!

Mortified, she allowed the pad and pen to clatter to the floor as she rubbed her throbbing temples. Twisting away, she moaned, "I'll leave immediately, naturally. Just—just don't fire Ivy."

"You're not from one of those tabloids?"

That question stopped her, for she'd already started toward the door. Still unable to look at him, she sagged against the cold wall. "No, no. I'm a teacher."

She heard him draw near, but couldn't move. "Who is this Harry?"

Her insides twisted and she shook her head. "Just let me go, Mr. Gallant." A tear trembled on her lower lashes, then slid down her cheek. Forlorn, she wiped it away.

She couldn't let him see her cry. Panicking, she started for the door again, but was halted by a hand on her shoulder. "Who the hell is Harry?" Though his tone was soft, there was a steely edge to his question. He meant to have an answer before she would be allowed to leave. "Why don't we go out onto my patio and talk?"

She resisted, shying away from his touch. "I'd rather—"

"What kind of a teacher are you?" This time he took her by the elbow, guiding her toward the window wall. The middle window opened at the touch of a hidden lever, and he stepped back, indicating that she precede him. "English? Math?"

She frowned in confusion, then realized he was asking about her occupation. Stepping onto a shady patio, she shook her head. "Biology."

He chuckled, and she peered at him. "What's so funny about teaching biology?"

He indicated a sitting area of two ornate cast iron love seats separated by a glass-topped coffee table. "Apparently you don't teach sex education, considering—"

"Can we get off that!" she cut in, surprised she could feel even more humiliated than she already did.

Like a prisoner being led to her execution, she headed toward the seating area. Surreptitiously she scanned her surroundings for possible avenues of escape. The patio was cozy and built of stone. The adjoining pool looked like a natural pond, set in the same rock as the patio. A waterfall poured from the hillside, spilling sparkling water into the pool's deep end. The cascading gurgle gave off a charming, serene sound that mingled with the twitter of birds.

It did truly seem like Eden amid the lushness of flowering tropical plants and exotic fruit trees. She recognized a few blossoms, the passion flower and a vivid medley of lilies, but much of the colorful foliage was foreign to her. The sultry summer air was heavy with sweet, musky scents, and she inhaled, somewhat calmed by nature's healing grandeur. In spite of her mood, she smiled as she took a seat in the shade of the house. "This is nice," she mused, unaware that she'd spoken until she heard her own comment.

"Thank you." Their gazes met, and he smiled lazily. "Should I hold off on burning it down?"

She lowered her glance to her lap, going tense. "Okay, so I'm no interior designer."

"You're a biology teacher with something against living in bank lobbies, I gather." He surprised her by sitting beside her. Casually he stretched an arm across the back of the love seat, his forearm brushing her nape. She shifted away from his touch, leaning against the metal arm, hoping he'd assume it was to better face him.

"Now, who is this Harry?"

She avoided his inquisitive eyes. Her perusal skittered about, to his powerful shoulders, his broad chest, the light blue knit shirt masking very little of his physique. He wore tan slacks, and her eyes were drawn down as he crossed an ankle on his other knee, his calf grazing her leg as he shifted. His shoes were beige tassel loafers that gave off the sheen of success.

She found herself staring at his bare, male ankle. It never occurred to her that a bastion of big business would go without socks. That sort of behavior seemed a bit nonconformist for a member of *Fortune's* Five Hundred, but she supposed Lyon Gallant was not a man to be dictated to, about socks or anything else.

As she drank in every tanned contour, she wondered if he had any idea that the skin and bones connecting his foot to his leg were such a blatant turn-on? Probably not. Nevertheless, it was a sin that this man had such charisma that even an ordinary hunk of flesh like an ankle became a stimulating feast for female eyes.

"Miss Stone?" he coaxed. "Are you that fascinated by my foot, or are you trying to avoid the subject?"

She snapped her gaze up, flushing. He'd been kidding about her interest in his foot, but unknowingly he'd been right. Fidgeting, she crossed her legs to put greater distance between them. His smile told her that her skittishness hadn't slipped by him. She doubted that much did.

"I really don't think Harry is your business," she tried, looking toward the waterfall.

"The fact that you're on my island under false colors makes it my business."

She didn't like to admit it, but he had a point. She realized she'd grabbed up wads of her skirt, and smoothed the fabric over her knees. "I—I suppose you do deserve an explanation."

"And that would be?"

"I..." This time she twisted completely away from him, grasping the metal arm of the love seat with both fists. "I..."

"You sound like a sailor."

She almost smiled at the unexpected joke, then merely shrugged. The story wasn't funny. "Harry was my—fiancé," she began falteringly. "We were to have been married on the twentieth of May. A week before that, my father died and my sister, Elsa, came home from New York for the funeral. While she was there, she and Harry—met, and then, on the day of our wedding, he—he and Elsa..." She shook her head, unable to go on.

The waterfall bubbled and gurgled in the drawn-out quiet. A flock of noisy, black and white plumed scaup streaked the sky above them, and was long gone before Lyon finally spoke. "So, this Harry ran off with your sister on your wedding day," he repeated, as though making sure he had his facts right. She detected no inflection in his tone.

Nodding, she clenched the metal until her fingers ached. Having to admit her failure as a woman was humiliating beyond her wildest dreams. Still, if it would keep Ivy from being fired, it had to be done.

"That's why you thought you needed to learn more about being sexy?" His voice was low, almost harsh. "To hold onto a man?"

Her head was bowed, her body slumped, but with his direct question, she jerked up, nausea rising in her throat. She wanted to cover her face with hands that were trembling badly, to scream, cry, give vent to her shame and disgrace, but she tried to hold on to her pride—just long enough to deny the awful truth.

Spinning, she glared at him, disconcerted to discover he was blurry before her. "No, I—" she began, but her breathing was coming so hard, so heavy, she couldn't talk. Pushing up from the bench, she broke eye contact and stepped away from him, knowing her tears had already given away the truth. "Okay—*okay*. It was stupid, I know, but I just thought..." Her words became a sob. She couldn't hold onto her composure one second longer. What did it matter? He was a bright man. He could put two and two together. "Please don't fire Ivy," she pleaded in a faulty whisper.

"Sit down, Miss Stone," he commanded softly.

She stiffened, resisting the order, but found that she was so shaky, it was the only choice she had. Though she did as he stipulated, she didn't look at him.

"And who is Mrs. Dillburg?"

Emily sniffed and was startled to find herself presented with a handkerchief. "Thanks," she mumbled, making loud use of it. "She's Ivy's niece. My best friend. She thought getting out of town would be good for me. And Ivy can't refuse Meg anything. So she let us come here." Dabbing at her eyes, she chanced a glimpse at him. His handsome mouth was thinned in displeasure, his eyes sharp and appraising. "They were just thinking of me," she added in a last-ditch effort to save Ivy's position.

He watched her for a long minute, his features grim, his eyes penetrating as though deciding if he believed her or not. After an interminable amount of time, he shook his head, one corner of his mouth twisting upward. "I thought you two were either the most thorough interior designers in the world, or the most inept."

She bit her lip, afraid to gather any hope. She couldn't tell from his expression if he believed her story, but at least he wasn't shoving her at gunpoint into the sea. "We'll leave today, Mr. Gallant," she promised in a whisper.

He crossed his arms before him, studying her for an additional moment. "No, you won't."

Fear gripped her again. "What are you saying?"

One brow rose in a shrug. "If I sent you away, I'd lose the best housekeeper I've ever had, because Ivy would quit. I can't have that."

She was amazed, and her expression no doubt reflected it, for his handsome features eased. "You're welcome to stay as long as you like." Surprising her, he stood, looking at his watch. When his glance returned to her face, he was all business. "I've got to go." He turned away, then stopped and shifted around, his dusky eyes speculative. "One thing. Did you want the sex lessons to get Harry back?"

She didn't know why she should be shocked by that question. She should be accustomed to his bluntness by now. Glancing away, she shook her head, very sure of her answer. "No. Not after..." She shrugged, unable to say it. When he didn't respond, she peeked at him. "Why?" She decided she had as much right to be blunt as he did.

"Because Harry doesn't deserve—" He stopped himself and pursed his lips as if to temper his remark. "Lesson four." With an odd little smile, he turned away. Seconds later he disappeared into his house, leaving her to ponder the message in his quiet remark. She'd never *had* lesson four. Surely he wasn't still suggesting they might...

She shivered, uncertain if it was dread or anticipation that engulfed her body. Surely it was dread. Surely she had no intention of allowing this playboy to make love to her!

*   *   *

Released from the lie, Meg and Emily accompanied Ivy to town the next two days in a row, more for Emily's benefit than Ivy's need. The women had taken Emily on as their pet project, insisting she buy clothes to better enhance her figure and her coloring. Emily had to admit that she felt more confident about herself, but it wasn't totally due to the transforming wardrobe. She'd learned things about herself in Lyon's capable arms. She'd seen real passion, real desire in his eyes, and she'd come to realize that even a man who'd known the most sensual women in the world could find her desirable. That knowledge gave her a new womanly power, a growing feeling of self-worth.

Still, she refused to buy any *Gallant's* underwear. Meg was fit to be tied when she couldn't explain her reasons. Or wouldn't. She didn't dare tell Meg that if she relented, she'd be giving in to her desire to attract him in his own arena, on his own terms. She wouldn't even think that way, let alone say it out loud. She would *not* be another sexual victory for Lyon Gallant's trophy case.

Meg took the defeat as well as she took any defeat. With nagging, ranting and more nagging. She went so far as to buy some, tossing it on Emily's bed almost challengingly. But Emily stuck the scanty things in a drawer and stood fast in her stick-in-the-mud decision, as Meg liked to call it.

Luckily, Lyon was having a party tonight, and they'd both been invited. That news had taken Meg's mind off the underwear war for the time being. Emily was grateful that thoughts of another gala evening had shifted her friend's thoughts away from undergarments. She decided not to muddy the waters by telling Meg she didn't intend to accept the invitation. Her friend would blow an artery.

At nine o'clock, the party had been going on for two hours. Emily could hear the music from where she wandered on a stretch of pristine beach. Some distance behind her she could see the great house, like a dark jewel gleaming in a setting of strategic outdoor illumination. More golden light spilled from every tall, arched window on the ground floor.

The mansion was a beguiling sight under the sun or the moon. Much like its owner. She felt foolishly sad as she stared, her heart wishing she was inside, dancing with the magnificent master of Sin Island. But her brain kept counseling her that it would be folly to allow herself to be so dangerously close to the man. His effect was instantaneous and all-consuming. Turning away, she reminded herself for the thousandth time that she was better off out here alone.

She heard distinct laughter, both masculine and feminine, then more voices. Some of the words were becoming too distinguishable for them to be drifting to her from the far away patio. Lurching around, she was shocked to see a throng of men and women clad in bathing suits heading in her direction. She gulped several times. It seemed the party she'd so carefully avoided was coming to her.

Lights flickered on in nearby palm trees, and Emily blinked, feeling like she'd been caught in an escape attempt from some high-security prison. Any second the alarm would sound and armed guards in helicopters would yell at her to drop to her face and spread-eagle on the sand.

"Em!" shouted Meg, making her jump. "Isn't this fun! Lyon decided to make it a swimming party. We're going to play volleyball, too."

Emily saw her friend waving as she hurried toward the beach, tugging along another woman. In fearful anticipation, Emily scanned the approaching crowd. There *he* was, and her heart leaped. She was filled with conflicting emotions. He was such an unfeeling tease, yet she was grateful for his kindness the other day, allowing her to stay on and caring about Ivy. Unfortunately, that just made it more imperative that she steer clear of him. She was so weak for his touch, it wouldn't take much to have her crying out for him to take her completely.

Unable to stop herself, she watched him stroll in her direction, clad in a low-slung swimsuit, his muscular chest, his taut belly and bulging thighs thrown in stunning relief under the lights illuminating the beach. He was sandwiched between two admiring women, each clinging to one of his arms.

"Em!" Meg cried again. "Look who I found!"

Emily dragged her gaze from her grinning host to focus on the willowy redhead before her. She did look familiar. When she managed to shove Lyon Gallant to a distant shelf in her mind, she realized she'd seen this woman before. "Didn't you do that rain forest special on the PBS station a couple of years ago?"

The woman looked startled, but seemed inordinately pleased. "Why, yes. You saw that?"

"It was wonderful. I've donated to saving the rain forest ever since. My name's Emily Stone."

"I'm Christmas Collier. I was always really proud of that piece."

Meg guffawed. "You would know her for that, Em. Anybody else in the world knows her from last winter's blockbuster movie, *Heaven's Fall*."

Emily shrugged sheepishly. "I'm sorry, Miss Collier. I don't get to movies much."

"Don't be sorry. Actually, that's how I met Lyon Gallant. He saw that special, too, and asked me to be in his catalogue."

Emily was startled that Lyon watched PBS. It didn't seem like something a lustful mover and shaker would do. But she supposed one of his people had told him to take a look at the woman, and he'd watched it for business reasons. "So, you're going to be in one of *Gallant's* catalogues?" she asked.

"I've been in several."

"Oh." Again, Emily felt terminally provincial. She *had* to get out more.

"Hey, they're setting up the volleyball net!" Meg dragged Christmas along, motioning at Emily. "Let's go, Em. Chris, did you know I was on the high school girl's varsity team?"

Emily smiled after her friend and answered Christmas's parting wave. She didn't bother to respond to Meg. Her friend was having so much fun she'd never know if Emily played volleyball or not.

"Hi, there." A nice-looking man of about thirty-five came up, and to Emily's surprise, was talking to her. "I don't remember meeting you inside." He grinned with obvious interest, something she wasn't used to. "I'm Kevin Etanburro. Art director of *Gallant's*." He took her hand in greeting.

"Hello." She didn't jump at his unexpected touch, and even managed an easy smile. She was surprised at herself. She'd done that with more self-confidence than she'd thought possible. At least not a couple of weeks ago.

"You must be new. I thought I'd met all the *Gallant's* models."

Emily blushed. "I'm just here visiting Ivy Dellin. I'm a teacher from Iowa."

He looked surprised. "You're not a model?" Glancing away, he shouted, "Hey, Lyon. Talk to you for a sec?"

Kevin was still holding her fingers. She didn't want to be rude, but she felt sure the handshake was over and tugged free. Besides, she didn't dare stick around if Lyon Gallant was coming over. From the look of it, he was disengaging himself from his female parasites and planning to do just that. "I'll leave you to talk to your boss."

"No, wait." He grasped her wrist to detain her. "I wanted to rake him over the coals for keeping you hidden."

She stared, baffled.

"What is it, Kev?" Lyon asked. Emily couldn't help but flick her gaze in his direction as he sauntered toward them through the low surf. He acknowledged her with a nod. "I see you've met Miss Stone."

The good-looking blond man grinned. "Hell, Lyon. She says she's a teacher from Iowa. Maybe we'd better check out Iowa the next time we need an all-America face and a drop-dead figure."

Emily could only gape, tongue-tied. Who were they talking about? Surely not *her*!

Lyon glanced her way, his grin making heat rise in her cheeks. "You might have a point."

"Could we use her in the December issue? Chris just told me she'd be in France on a movie set then."

Her host's gaze roamed over her swimsuit-clad body. "Whatever the lady says."

The blond man winked at his boss. "I never get a refusal. You know that."

Lyon eyed Kevin's hand holding hers, his lips twitching wryly. "Never say never, Kev." Glancing at Emily, he nodded cordially. "Nice to have you join us at last, Miss Stone." His gaze only lingered for one more second, but it was long enough for her to detect amusement. He was making the point that he was well aware she *hadn't* joined the party, that she'd been drawn in against her will— and, last but not least, he knew Kevin was about to get his very first rejection.

How dare he be so damned all-knowing! It would serve him right if she didn't refuse! She stiffened as he shifted his broad shoulders around and walked to where the volleyball game was getting under way.

There was a tug on her fingers. "What about it, Miss Stone? You'd get a thousand dollars for the shoot."

She swiveled around, overwhelmed. "A *what*?"

He grinned. "A thousand. And you keep the underwear you model, naturally."

Her eyes widened. "A thousand dollars?" That was two weeks salary for her! But the fact about the big money was stunted by his other statement—that she'd be modeling Gallant's underwear. Even if Lyon deserved to be wrong about her, never in a million years did she plan to wear that microscopic underwear. She couldn't possibly be seen in a magazine that millions of people read— probably even some of her students!

"I—I..." She demurely withdrew her hand from his, smiling to assuage her refusal. "I'm sure that's a wonderful opportunity, Mr...." She couldn't remember his last name, so she amended, "Kevin. It's just that I don't think modeling underwear is exactly my—well, I do teach young people."

He grinned good-naturedly. "Damn lucky kids." Taking her by the arm, he led her toward the volleyball game. "We'll talk about it later over a drink. Let's work up a thirst."

Emily had to admit the volleyball game was fun, and Kevin was attentive and amusing company. He helped her learn to serve the ball and taught her how to bat it over the net. She wasn't half bad. Even though Lyon's team won, she felt like a victor, anyway. She'd tried something and had a good time.

The game was over but for a few diehards. She waded knee-deep in lapping surf at the edge of the light, while Kevin trekked the long distance to the patio to get her a cup of punch. For the first time since the invasion of partyers she was standing alone, enjoying the tropical night.

"So, are we going to see you on the cover of *Gallant's*?"

She recognized Lyon's voice and reacted strongly but tried not to show it. "I thought I'd try going naked in *Playboy* first," she quipped.

He laughed softly. "Kevin means it, you know." She faced him, which was a mistake. His smile was arresting, his eyes somehow softer, more approving in this light. "You are lovely, sweetheart."

The low admission melted strategic bones in her body, and she felt unsteady. His sporadic use of an endearment instead of her name was driving her crazy. "Why do you do that?" she asked, her voice thready.

"What?"

He drew nearer, exuding a sensual heat that was disorienting. "Um, sometimes you call me Miss Stone, and sometimes you call me sweetheart. Why?"

"Why do you think?"

The noises of the party began to fade, and she knew it was because he had the power to absorb every ounce of her senses. Breathing became difficult, and she inhaled then exhaled quickly, almost panting. "I—I think you need to find a hobby."

He grinned. "Did you know you were smiling that smile I taught you at Kevin?"

She was startled by the change of subject. "What smile?"

"That sly, I'd-love-to-knee-Lyon-Gallant smile. I'm flattered you were thinking of me."

She was taken off guard by the joke and grinned in spite of herself. "You're welcome. Happy to do it."

"It worked, too. He's crazy for you."

She blinked, startled. When she found her voice, she rasped, "Don't be silly."

He cupped her chin with his fingers. Brushing a light kiss on her lips, he murmured, "I'm never silly, sweetheart."

He'd started to walk away before she could find her voice. "Why do you do that?"

"Kiss you?" He shifted. His eyes were narrowed and he seemed annoyed with himself.

She licked her lips, trying to wipe away the taste of him. He couldn't be any more annoyed about it than she was. Working at remembering her question, she cried, "No—

why do you call me Miss Stone sometimes and sweetheart sometimes?''

He half grinned, but without much humor. ''Because sometimes you are Miss Stone, and sometimes—like just now, when you looked so astonished that a man could find you desirable—you're a sweetheart.''

He shrugged, muscles rippling with the act. ''I supposed I kissed you because I found that quality irresistible.'' He turned to fully face her, his gaze growing so penetrating she felt naked before him.

When he bent toward her in a confiding way it took all her willpower not to throw her arms about his neck and beg him to make love to her. ''He'll kiss you tonight,'' he whispered, his eyes searching hers, his smile gone. Tension coiled in her stomach in anticipation. She had a sense he had something even more shocking to say. ''He would make love to you, too, if you'd let him.''

She stared, unable to comprehend such an outrageous prediction, let alone respond to it.

He watched her stupefaction, and his eyes began to glint with amusement. ''But you won't let him, will you.''

It hadn't been a question. He was stating the facts as he knew them and seemed satisfied with his wisdom on the subject of the inhibited Emily Stone. She shifted uncomfortably under his shrewd stare, suddenly incensed that she was so sexually predictable. She hadn't made much headway in her quest to change.

Her pride was stung, and she lifted her chin. "I don't know what I'll do about Kevin, Mr. Gallant. Of course, he *is* terribly cute, and I've always loved blondes," she lied, deciding he deserved to be taken down a peg or two, the arrogant egotist. "Since you brought it up," she said sweetly, warming to the fiction, "I think Kevin would be a perfect teacher for—lesson four. Don't you agree?"

His eyes narrowed slightly, as though he was considering this new twist. "I wouldn't know. I've never made love to the man."

She laughed, finding his sarcasm truly funny. "Well." She shrugged, tossing her curls in as frivolous manner as she could manage. "Since it's your island, I suppose I could let you know how it went—in the morning."

One dark brow arched and he seemed about to say something when movement caught his eye and he flicked his glance toward shore. "Your date's coming back." His features unreadable, he studied her face for another heartbeat, then turned away. He muttered something she was sure she must have misunderstood, for it sounded like, "Harry was a damned fool."

As she stared, unblinking, he went away, taking her heart with him.

Kevin sloshed to her side, handing her a cup of red liquid. Her smile came only with great effort, for it was at that instant she discovered she'd fallen in love with Lyon Gallant—a man who had no apparent problem with the idea that she might end up sleeping with a friend of his that very night.

CHAPTER SEVEN

EMILY'S heart and mind were in such turmoil she couldn't sleep. And she was starving. She'd skipped dinner, since it was part of Lyon's gala party, and the glass of punch she'd had with Kevin hadn't been very filling. She shook her head, recalling how hard it had been to finally convince her ardent companion that she wasn't going to model in *Gallant's*, and she wasn't going to bed with him, either.

He'd taken it like a gentleman, but to Emily's surprise, he'd asked for her phone number and address back in Iowa. She had a feeling he'd call. Strange, she thought. She'd spent her life being the retiring wallflower hardly anyone had ever asked to dance. Apparently she'd put out don't-touch-me signals all those years. She hadn't meant to, she'd just been afraid of doing or saying something wrong.

Consequently, she'd buried herself in her studies, making learning her life. Maybe she thought if she studied, she'd learn how to be free and easy with people. It hadn't worked that way. She'd just felt more and more abnormal, less and less confident.

Then Lyon Gallant had come along with his kisses and his husky passion, showing her how much of a woman she could be under the right guidance. Amazingly, Kevin had detected something alluring in her—and that *something* she knew she owed to Lyon's skilled tutelage.

Her stomach growled, and she exhaled tiredly. She simply had to eat. Even though it was one o'clock in the morning, and even though she'd gained a touch of spontaneity and self-assurance, she still hadn't given herself over completely to wild abandon. So she decided she'd better change from her nightgown into real clothes if she intended to go wandering around the house. She chose a skirt and blouse she'd bought yesterday, deciding to try them out in the dead of night when nobody could see her.

The white cotton corset top was reminiscent of Victorian underwear, though by today's standards it was pretty tame. She slipped it on and laced it up the front, tying the ribbon at the low, square-cut neckline. Then she stepped into the full, circle skirt of blue and white checks.

She didn't know why, but as she slipped into thong sandals, she inspected herself in the mirror, fluffing curls nearly dry from the shower. She shook her head at herself, watching bright ringlets dance across her eyes. Pushing them back, she smiled wryly. This wasn't the Emily who'd come here three weeks ago. This Emily was sleeker from her jogging, tanned, with bouncy, almost defiant hair. Sun-streaked with blond highlights, it curved and crinkled around her heart-shaped face in luminous disarray, giving her a tempestuous look. She wasn't sure she totally approved of it, but it clearly had an effect on men.

She scanned herself from head to toe, feeling a flush creep up her cheeks. Thanks to Ivy's trips into Miami with them, and Meg's incessant bossing about clothes, she could actually see this Emily's figure. And this Emily had an interesting new glint in her eyes. Was it a touch of self-assurance? Before she allowed herself to look too closely, her glance plummeted to the floor. Maybe she was gaining a little self-confidence, but she didn't dare search deeper in the sapphire depths or she would also see sadness.

It was ironic how the same self-satisfied egotist could be responsible for both manifestations in her eyes. Heaving a sigh, she spun away from the mirror. Maybe she'd feel better when she had something in her stomach.

Moments later, she pushed through the door to the big, utilitarian kitchen, all white and stainless steel, and was stunned to see Lyon there. He was alone. His back was to her, and he was clad only in sweatpants. Standing before the stove, he had stilled in stirring something, but didn't turn when he heard the door. "No! I told you ten minutes ago I don't want you to fix me anything," he growled. "And, no, I still don't want to be served in my suite. And, no, I don't need you to come wake me for my six o'clock meeting."

It startled Emily to see this commanding man upset. He'd set down his spatula and planted his palms flat on the stainless steel surface, hunching his shoulders as though frustrated and trying to maintain control.

"Is that understood?" he demanded.

For some reason, rather than frightening or intimidating her, his agitation seemed endearing. It was her first glimpse into his unguarded, human side.

"Well..." She walked toward the long white kitchen table that separated them. "First, it looks like somebody besides you ought to do your cooking, because I smell smoke."

He shifted around, his scowl becoming surprise as she went on with a fledgling smile. "Secondly, I have no intention of serving you—anyplace. And third, if you have a six o'clock meeting, I have a feeling you're going to yawn all the way through it."

He regained himself quickly and leaned against the stove, crossing his legs at the ankles. She noticed he was barefoot. Nice feet, she mused, then gritted her teeth against such a wayward thought.

He inclined his head, a brow rising in question. "Your midnight cha-cha with Kev over already?"

She came up before him and gave him a rankled look. "Move. Let me see what you're incinerating."

He shifted away, but didn't go far. His heady scent was strong in her nostrils, stimulating, even mixed with the charred smell of burned eggs.

"You didn't answer my question," he reminded her.

"You know the answer to that as well as you already knew I wouldn't model in your catalogue."

"But you told me—"

"You were so darned smug, thinking you knew everything about me," she broke in. "Pride made me say that."

He didn't speak while she scraped at the pile of scrambled eggs, to no avail. When his lack of response drew out so long she couldn't stand the quiet anymore, she tried to get back on track, asking, "Is this the way you like your eggs or should we start over?"

"We?"

She looked at him. He wasn't quite smiling, but the irritation was gone from his features. "I'm starving. I missed dinner, you know."

"And who's fault was that?" This time his lips curved slightly.

She ignored the question and handed him the pan. "Put this in the sink. When it cools we can soak it. Meanwhile, I'll get more eggs."

"I used them all up," he said as he took away the skillet.

"I bet we can find something eatable in this joint."

He chuckled. "There's leftover roast."

"Sandwiches." She headed for the huge refrigerator. "You find bread."

"You're pretty bossy in the middle of the night."

She'd opened the refrigerator but turned to look at him. Lifting her chin, she smirked. "And I bet you're a lousy cook anytime of the day or night. By the way, who did you think you were talking to when I came in?"

He crossed his arms, lounging against the white-tiled counter. "I thought you were one of the household staff." He shrugged. "They can't stand the idea of my doing anything myself."

She shook her head in mock distress. "It must be hell for you." She bent to retrieve the needed ingredients. When she turned around, he was standing beside her. He took the roast and condiments from her fingers before she recovered from her shock. "Must you sneak up on me?" she finally managed.

"I'm sorry. Wooden floors and bare feet tend to cause quiet approaches."

"No." She rejected that explanation, following him to a long expanse of counter. "Bare feet make slapping sounds on wood floors."

He looked at her, his eyes sparkling. "Who do you live with, Daffy Duck?"

She smiled, startled at herself for being so at ease. It was probably because there wasn't a moon above them. Or, more likely, because once Lyon Gallant kissed you, you could never be all business with him again, even if you wanted to. "So your staff hates to see you burn eggs?"

"I don't usually burn them. I was just..."
He frowned, his glance shifting away almost
guiltily. "Thinking."

"That can be dangerous." She opened the
bread and shoved it in front of him. "I've
seen Meg try it. Scary. Here, you spread the
mustard."

His frown disappeared and he took up a
knife. "I like your outfit."

For some reason his compliment disconcerted her. Maybe it was because he was so
close, or because his eyes held a lush glimmer.
Hoping he wasn't thinking about getting her
naked and introducing her to lesson four, she
quickly switched the subject. "Uh, I'd say
you're a prisoner of your own success,
wouldn't you?"

He halted and peered at her. "That's quite
a switch. What do you mean?"

She got to work slicing roast beef so she
wouldn't have to meet his gaze. "You don't
even have the freedom to burn eggs when you
feel like it."

She cast a glance at his hands. They weren't
moving, his sandwich-making forgotten.
"Nothing's perfect, Miss Stone."

He'd said it as though his jaws were clenched. "Oh, dear, you called me Miss Stone." Setting down her knife, she peeked at him. "Tell me, Mr. Gallant. What exactly would be perfect?"

He squinted, looking away as though in thought. "More success, I suppose."

"More!" She was aghast. "More?" she repeated, unbelieving. "How could you want more than you have?"

He looked at her, his eyes filling with icy reproach. "There's no such thing as enough."

She felt as though she'd been hit in the stomach, and all the air left her body. "How can you—where did you . . ."

He smiled, but it wasn't pleasant. "Dear old Dad taught me, 'The man who dies with the most toys wins.'"

She blinked. "Your father?"

He swiped mustard on the bread without much notice. "Dad was never a happy person. Never had the recognition he wanted and needed for his ego. Never had the time for me until I took over his little catalogue business and made him rich."

She was surprised to discover that she and the all-powerful Lyon Gallant had childhoods in common—an overbearing father and a desire for his approval. Feeling a rush of soft kinship for him, she asked, "Where is your father?"

"He died four years ago." Lyon looked her way briefly, his nostrils flaring. "But he was rich."

She began to slice beef again, listlessly, her appetite gone. "And was he happy?"

His chuckle was edged with bitterness. "Happier than when he was poor."

"Did he love you more after you made him rich?"

He slanted a dark gaze at her, his eyes flashing offense. "He knew I was alive."

Her heart went out to him. How many times in her life had her father made it clear that her sister, Elsa, was his favorite? How many times had she done everything, *anything* he'd asked of her to win his approval? It was only after Elsa ran away to New York to become an artist that he acknowledged Emily as worthy of his attention at all. Becoming a teacher had helped, too, but nothing was ever quite enough. He'd mourned Elsa's loss until the day he died.

Emily had an urge to take Lyon's hand, to hug him—one lonely little girl comforting one lonely little boy. Unfortunately, they weren't children anymore. They were adults. And she'd already been in his arms, already knew the insanity of such an act, no matter how well-meant. Trying to turn her mind to safer subjects, she took the bread slices he'd prepared and placed lettuce on them, then added meat. "Where's your mother?"

"She died when I was three. I don't remember her."

Emily's hands faltered in her work. It seemed as though Lyon Gallant's luck with parents had been worse than hers. At least she'd had her mother's love and support for fifteen years.

"What about relationships? Or do you think of women as toys, too?" She bit the inside of her cheek, wishing she hadn't let that question slip out. But her heart had to know.

"I think of women as beautiful, willing toys."

She closed her eyes for a split second, then gathered her poise. "I must have been a tedious change of pace for you." She turned away, swallowing to ease the lump of despair in her throat. Straining to keep her voice placid, she said, "I like tomatoes on my sandwich. Do you have any?"

"Damned if I know."

"I'm sure the staff won't mind if I check." She headed to the refrigerator, forcing her mind to food and off Lyon's callous outlook on life. "Do you want any?"

"Why not?"

After she'd checked several crisper drawers, she found tomatoes and grabbed one. When she turned around, he was there, plucking the fruit from her fingers. He grinned, and this time she was sure she saw seduction in his gaze. "You weren't all that tedious, sweetheart. I told you once tonight that you're beautiful. You just have old-fashioned morals."

She sidestepped and closed the refrigerator door, her heart hammering. She wanted him to take her into his arms—yet she didn't want it. Her emotions were so chaotic she was hard-pressed not to shriek and run from the room. "And—and you have the cure for old-fashioned morals, I suppose?"

"Now that you mention it."

She took the tomato from his hand and hurried to where the sandwiches waited. Picking up the knife, she slashed through the tomato several times before realizing she was using the dull side. By then, it was too late. The tomato looked like it had been hit by a train.

"We have a juicer," he commented dryly. "I thought you wanted slices."

Nervously, she scooped up the glop from the cutting board and piled it onto their sandwiches. "You'll love it this way," she muttered, slapping a slice of bread on top of the dripping mess. "They're ready."

He picked up the plates and carried them to the table. "Now, about my virginity cure..." He set the plates side by side on the table.

She stilled. "I never said I was a virgin!"

He flashed her a knowing grin. "You said it in a thousand ways, sweetheart." Pulling a chair out for her, he indicated that she take a seat. "I've kissed you, remember?"

She was mortified, but she was also insulted. Snatching up her plate, she marched to the opposite side of the table. she had no idea why, for there was no way she could eat now. Her stomach was churning with embarrassment. Why didn't she just leave? "I'm so inept, I should put myself in an old virgin's home! Is that it?" She pulled out a chair and plopped down, but her glare didn't waver from his face.

"You could take the cure," he reminded her after seating himself.

Her glare became a wide-eyed stare. "If you'll remember, you already tried your cure. I was too inhibited."

He leaned forward, his forearms on the table, his long, tanned fingers very near hers. She dropped her hands into her lap to safeguard herself against doing something stupid like grabbing him and begging for his love.

Even though they weren't making physical contact, his gaze caught and held hers, affecting her breathing. "You're not inhi-

bited,'' he assured softly. ''Just inexperi-
enced.''

She colored fiercely. It had almost seemed
like he meant that. His tone, his eyes, the way
his hands rested on the table, ready to take
hers if she would only allow it. She scanned
his face again, looking for signs of teasing and
deceit, but she could see nothing but truth.
Heavens! He'd meant it! Everything about
him told her he'd really meant it. Her heart
flip-flopped with alarm and exultation.

''If you'd like we could try lesson four
again.''

She listened to his soft urging, looked into
his seductive eyes. She wanted lesson four
from him more than anything, but she knew
if he made love to her, she would never, never
be able to go on with her life as though it had
meant nothing.

He'd already told her women to him were
playthings. Pleasant, willing playthings. She
clutched her hands together in her lap. She
couldn't just be his *toy*. ''I—I don't want you
to make love to me,'' she lied through gritted
teeth, hoping she sounded more convincing
than she felt.

"Ouch." He grunted out a humorless laugh and shook his head. "You really know how to hurt a guy."

"I'm sure the pain will go away. The world is full of willing toys."

He inclined his head, examining her dubiously. "Let me get this straight. You want to learn about lovemaking so you can be sexy, but your morals keep getting in the way. Right?"

When she nodded, he pursed his lips.

She sagged against the back of her chair. "I suppose it's crazy to think I can have it both ways." This conversation was sordid and outrageous. She felt like such a stupid fool for even being here.

"I have a solution," he said quietly. When her gaze snapped up, his brows lifted in sly challenge. "It's a little crude, but it's helped thousands of women lose their virginity all over the world."

"You must really get around," she muttered.

At her sarcasm, his lips split, showing off one dashing dimple. "I've had a lot of help. Care to try?"

"It doesn't involve making love?"

He shrugged. "Not in the strictest sense."

He was so worrisomely good-looking with that erotic half-grin, she could feel her resolve slipping. But how could this possibly work—making love without making love? "No, I don't..." She shook her head, but the lie was sour on her tongue. She *did* want to know. And his probing expression told her he knew it. Ashamed of herself for her weakness, she inhaled raggedly. "Okay—what is it?"

He watched her for a few seconds, his twisted smile remaining intact, though his brow knitted slightly. When he wordlessly pushed up to stand, she stiffened with anticipation. It was impossible for him to make love to her without making love to her. So, in a few seconds, Lyon Gallant would take her into his capable arms. He had just eased into it using sneaky semantics. And right now, she didn't care how he'd worked it, she just knew something deep inside her needed his touch, and her need was a thousand times greater than her fear of the consequences.

He didn't circle the table and pull her into his embrace as she'd expected. Instead, he went to a cabinet and took a bottle from the top shelf, then retrieved a tumbler from another. When he came back, he uncapped the bottle and filled the glass with a liquid that looked like weak tea. "Drink this." He thumped the glass and bottle on the table and shoved them across at her.

She sniffed and frowned at him, dismayed. "It's alcoholic."

"Right." He sat back, crossing his arms over a bare chest that was incredibly male. "Ten minutes after you down that Scotch, you'll be too soused to stand up, let alone have any inhibitions. When you can't remember your name, we'll have sex here on the table." He lifted a casual shoulder. "Then goodbye old-fashioned morals."

She sat there, blank, dazed. He was talking to her with such cool nonchalance about something that should be meaningful between two people, she couldn't believe her ears.

When she didn't respond, he lifted his arm and peered at his watch. "Drink, Miss Stone. Remember, I have an early meeting in the morning."

She let out a gasp, anger draining the blood from her face. "You have a—a *meeting*?" she rasped. "I have to get drunk so we can get rid of my pesky morals, and on top of that I have to *hurry* because you have a meeting?" A thought whipped into her brain so quickly she hardly had time to absorb it, let alone decide if it was smart or not. But she was too hurt to analyze it.

Glaring at him, she jumped up. "Well, I certainly don't want to keep you waiting! Not even ten minutes!" Shoving the bottle and tumbler aside, they crashed to the tile floor as she hiked up her skirt and dropped a knee on the table. His complacent features grew troubled when she crawled onto the tabletop and swept the plates out of the way. They clattered and clanked, sliding to the other end of the long surface, but by some miracle, they didn't fall. "We can forget the drinking part— *sweetheart*!" she hissed. "That would cut into your precious time. Let's just get my pesky morals out of the way." Sitting down hard, she lowered herself to her back and clutched the sides of the table. "Okay, Mr. I

Have a Meeting! *Do* me! Let's get it over with!''

His face showed concerned surprise as he pushed himself up in a strange slow motion. She felt a twitter of amusement at his expense. For once she could laugh at *his* shock! It was obvious he'd been taunting her again. Mocking her. Knowing she couldn't go through with such a bloodless suggestion. The bum! Well, she'd had enough of his superior attitude, thinking he knew so much about her midwestern morals. She'd show him! He didn't know what a truly angry, determined Iowa girl was capable of when pushed too far!

He towered beside her, unmoving. ''What the hell do you think you're doing?''

''I'm waiting! Time's wastin', buster. Jump my bones, then go to your *pressing* meeting.''

With narrowed eyes, he scanned her stiffened body from head to toe.

''You've lost a sandal,'' he muttered.

''That's not all I'm going to lose!'' she reminded him through clamped jaws. ''Why are you stalling?''

His nostrils flared, but after only another millisecond's hesitation, he walked to the end of the table. When he got there, he unceremoniously removed her remaining sandal and tossed it to the floor. The sizzling touch of his hand on her foot sent a bolt of electricity through her and she stopped breathing. She glanced at his face. He wasn't smiling, and the muscles in his cheeks bunched in agitation. "You want the lights on or off?"

"On!" She hiked her chin with false bravado. "Or are you intimidated by lights?"

"I'm fine with the lights." His eyes flashed with consternation.

Good lord, he was untying his sweatpants! She went suddenly light-headed, and her heart constricted painfully.

After loosening the ties, he held them in his fists, his thunderous expression chilling her to her core. "You'll have to let go of the table to lift your skirt," he growled.

She was stunned by his surliness. "Don't— don't you want to?"

"I'm 'doing you,' not making love to you, remember?"

That scornful reminder crushed her. Suddenly she felt cheap and dirty. He was standing there, ready to drop his pants, but his only touch had been to get rid of her shoe. She stared at him. Dark tendrils of hair fell across his wrinkled brow, and his lips were drawn down in umbrage. Her hands tingled with an urge to touch his thick, velvety hair, to languidly caress it hour upon hour. And she ached to feel the passionate heat of his mouth against hers, drawing her away from the earth toward heaven.

This wasn't the way it was supposed to be! This was so heartless. Her lips began to tremble, and she pulled them between her teeth to try to hide her torment. A slanderous tear slid from the corner of her eye and trailed into the curls at her temple. It was too late. There was no hiding her misery now. She might as well say what she felt. "I—I was wrong about your bedroom being too cold," she cried weakly. "It's *perfect* for you."

She didn't think his eyes could get any harder, but they did. Like slivers of polished jet. His raw blasphemy made her flinch. Knotting the ties of his pants, he stalked to her side. Peeling her fingers from around the tabletop, he pulled her up to sit. "Take your morals and go back to Iowa, Miss Stone,'' he ground out.

He stared at her, looking as though he wanted to berate her further. But he didn't. Scraping a hand testily through his hair, he gritted another curse, then stalked out of the kitchen.

She sat for a long time staring at her sandal, laying on its side where he'd tossed it. Caustic fumes of the spilled Scotch burned her nose and stung her eyes. But her tears had nothing to do with that.

Lyon Gallant couldn't have made his attitude any clearer if he'd put her on a plane himself. She could never be the kind of woman he wanted. And he had no intention of being the kind of man she needed.

It was too bad that knowledge didn't make the pain of loving him thud less severely in her chest.

Meg fell backward onto Emily's bed, covering her face with her hands and wailing theatrically. ''So, you're saying you wouldn't let Lyon make love to you and you wouldn't let him, uh, initiate you, either? And he offered to do *both*?"

Emily wearily lowered herself to her dresser bench. She'd only managed to keep her awful secret for four days, and with Meg's aghast expression, she wished she'd sewn her mouth shut. "I knew I should never have confided in you." She laced her fingers and clenched them into a ball in her lap.

Meg rolled on her side to scowl at her friend. "Em, honey, wake up and smell the nineties before they're over!" She pushed up, so agitated she couldn't be still for a second. "You wanna know how I lost my virginity?"

"You lost it on your wedding night with Larry."

"No, I didn't. I never told you the truth because I knew you'd have a cow." Meg fell back again, staring at the ceiling. "I was sixteen, and let's just say it wasn't to a handsome millionaire under a tropical moon. More like a rattletrap pickup truck on a muddy country road. I probably still have the gearshift scars on my—"

"Meg!" Emily interrupted, disquieted by the bombshell. "You're not helping."

The petite brunette vaulted up so quickly Emily almost fell off the bench in surprise. "Look, Em," Meg cried, exasperation sharpening her tone. "I've *been* helping. I've been a good and true friend! I got you out of town, talked the most straitlaced woman in creation to *lie* so we could come here! What more can I do than I've already done?"

Emily was abashed, squeezing her hands into a tighter ball. Meg was right. She'd been as good a friend as she knew how to be.

"It's only *sex*," Meg insisted. "You're not murdering anybody!" She came over to perch on the bench beside Emily and seized her hands. "Em, remember when you took that frog class in college?"

Emily was confused for a moment, then understood. "The evolution of amphibians?"

"Whatever." Meg waved a dismissing hand. "You hated the professor, but you knew you needed to know the stuff and he was the best teacher. Right?" She squeezed Emily's fingers. "What's so different about this? You've always pursued wisdom and education. What's your problem now? You need to know about being sexy. Lyon's the best teacher—maybe in the whole *world*! He's willing! Can't you think of it as another course you need?''

Emily averted her gaze. ''But—but he's so...'' She couldn't tell Meg she'd fallen in love with him and that his casual attitude about sex and women was too distressing to deal with—let alone experience. *And have to remember for the rest of her life.* She hedged. ''He's just not—my type.''

Meg made a disgruntled sound. ''Impossible! That's like saying breathing doesn't agree with you.''

Emily couldn't argue with that and lowered her gaze to the Oriental rug. Her friend's glowering face was too hard to look at. Withdrawing her hands from Meg's, she sighed. ''Besides, I don't think he's willing anymore. I've rejected him too much.''

''You're probably right. Why should he waste his time—'' She paused, and Emily looked up in time to see her screw up her face, looking contrite. ''Sorry, Em. I didn't mean it the way it sounded.''

Emily laughed ruefully. ''Sure, you did. Why should he waste time on a reluctant schoolteacher when beautiful models and superstars are throwing themselves at him.''

Meg patted Emily's arm encouragingly. ''Well, if that's the way it is, then you should try somebody else.''

Emily was so stunned by Meg's single-mindedness she couldn't imagine she'd heard right. ''What?''

Meg's shrug was unperturbed. ''Aunt Ivy told me Lyon's having his legal department over for a party tomorrow. Naturally we're invited. I bet there'll be a dozen good-looking lawyers roaming around.'' She stared hard into Emily's eyes, as though trying to force her will directly into her brain. ''You'll look them all over and then...'' She winked. ''Then—let the one you like best know you're available.''

Emily gaped, nonplussed. She couldn't believe she'd heard what she just heard. ''Tell me, Meg, as a child did you eat a lot of paint?''

Meg's guffaw filled the room. ''I know you're surprised by the idea, but think about it. It's perfect!''

''It's terrible!''

Meg's face fell as though she'd been slapped. "You're *impossible*!" She jumped up, throwing her hands in the air. "I give up! Go ahead, be America's oldest virgin! Maybe they'll build a statue to you, and you can cuddle up to *that* on cold nights!"

Emily stared, stunned by her friend's hateful tone. Meg was fed up, and that knowledge wounded her deeply. Scanning her friend's pinched face, Emily felt misery ooze from her every pore. It suddenly seemed as though she was mourning the death of both a friendship and a mission. The first was too important to her to lose, the other too trifling to fight about in this day and age. Meg had gone above and beyond the call of duty, with only Emily's best interest at heart. And how had she repaid her? By acting like a prude and a coward. After all, what Meg said was true—it was only sex.

Swallowing hard, she made her decision hastily, knowing that was the only way to finally do it—fast and without deep thought. That had always been her problem. She thought too much. Girls lost their virginity all the time, just to have it over and done. She'd heard her own students whispering about just such plans as though they were talking about going to the movies! She was twenty-four, for heaven's sake. Her turn was way overdue.

Rocketing up from her seat, she grasped Meg by the shoulders and made a solemn vow with her eyes. "Okay, tomorrow I'll pick out a handsome young lawyer and—and just do it."

"No kidding?" With Emily's resolute nod, Meg's face lit in a grin. "Operation Lay a Lawyer is underway!" She planted an enthusiastic kiss on Emily's cheek and flounced out of the room.

Feeling strangely drained, Emily trudged to her bed and sprawled on her face. "Operation Lay a Lawyer," she mumbled into the bedspread. Closing her eyes, she pressed her hands to her temples, not a bit surprised a harrowing headache had sprung to life in her forehead.

CHAPTER EIGHT

THE early morning quiet was destroyed when
Emily heard the roar of the big helicopter
coming in for a landing. Hastily she decided
to change her jogging route. She hadn't seen
Lyon since the scene in the kitchen five nights
ago, and she didn't care to see him until it was
absolutely necessary—if at all. She spun
around, intent on racing down the beach the
way she'd come, but she came to a stumbling
halt.

The master of Sin Island couldn't be
landing on his island this morning because he
was strolling along a pathway leading out of
the woods. Since he was coming directly
toward her, she didn't have a chance to escape
unnoticed. Uneasily she scanned him, the
sight of his bare chest and shoulders trig-
gering a disconcerted frown. He was clad only
in cutoffs and work boots. His tool belt hung
low on trim hips, and he carried the infamous
toolbox she'd so gracelessly tumbled over the

first time they'd met. No doubt he was on his way back from working on his cabin in the cove.

He didn't smile at her. When he was within a few feet, he halted and nodded, his eyes silently appraising. "Morning, Miss Stone."

She frantically pulled herself together. Though she was short of breath from his unexpected appearance and her jog, she was determined to explain something that had been preying on her mind. "Look, Mr. Gallant. My airline ticket is nonrefundable. I can't fly back to Plattville for three more days. I'm sorry, but I can't afford to throw away a five-hundred-dollar ticket."

His brows dipped. "I didn't mean you had to leave my island. I just meant you shouldn't force yourself to be what you can't be." He cast a glance behind her toward the distant helipad. "I need to get changed. My guests are arriving."

She took the statement as a dismissal and started to sprint away from him when the sound of her name halted her. Reluctantly, she turned back.

"There's going to be a picnic on the beach this afternoon. Do you plan to attend?"

She shrugged, unsmiling, but remembered her promise to Meg. "I suppose...yes."

He lifted his chin in a half nod, his features giving away neither pleasure nor irritation. "I'll see you then."

"I'll try not to get in your way."

His teeth flashed, and even as brief and derisive as the grin was, it took away her breath. "Don't worry, sweetheart. You won't."

Though she'd intended to make a hurried escape, she couldn't seem to move as he turned and walked away. Heaving a sigh, she shook her head. His remark could be taken two ways, but she supposed after their last disastrous encounter she could only believe the scathing interpretation. He wouldn't notice if she was there or not because he'd marked her off his list of inhibited schoolteachers to give sex lessons to. She knew she should be grateful for that. The tragedy was—she was devastated.

Straightening with difficulty, she cast a helpless gaze toward the sky. "You'd better get changed, too, Emily,'' she muttered, her voice cracking. ''You have a lawyer to...''

Just because she couldn't say the word didn't change anything. She'd promised Meg. She'd promised herself. And today was her day of reckoning!

It was no picnic like Emily had ever seen or imagined. A band was set up at the edge of the beach, under the shade of tall, feathery ferns and palms. They were playing popular soft rock to the attendant harmony of hissing surf and songbirds. Glossy coquina shells glinted in the sun like uncovered pirate's treasure. A few brave pelicans, looking like prehistoric reptiles, skimmed the glimmering ocean or glided overhead to gawk at the human invasion.

Emily was sitting alone at one of the more obscure of ten card tables that had been set up on the beach. Each had been covered with a white linen cloth and had a centerpiece of fresh-cut flowers in a crystal vase. From her shady vantage point on the edge of the festivities, she dug her toes into the cool sand, inhaling the smell of sea salt and algae, mingled with the aroma of grilling steaks.

A long table farther back on the lawn was loaded down with boiled shrimp, lobster, crab, oysters on the half shell and smoked salmon. Tons of fancy hors d'oeuvres were on the table, along with plates of colorful melon and other exotic fruit.

The steaks, as well as delicacies not yet on display, would be the main course, but Emily wasn't hungry. Though she toyed with a serving of delicious pineapple seasoned with fresh mint, she couldn't manage to eat much. She was too aware of what she must do. Uneasily, she surveyed the assembled guests, her stomach knotting with fear.

There were certainly enough handsome lawyers in the Gallant legal department. Meg had made it her duty to cull the married from the unmarried. Her whispered reports revealed that there were five single males to choose from in a department of twenty lawyers.

Now all Emily had to do was decide which of the five would suit her purposes the best. That might not be as difficult as she at first feared. Three of the men had made it obvious that they were interested in getting to know her better. One of those was heading her way now, his plate piled high with shrimp.

She sat back in her lawn chair, trying to appear relaxed and receptive. Taking a sip of cola, she watched his leisurely approach. Not quite six feet tall, he was stocky, like a football player. His hair was light brown and slightly thinning. His face was nice, his features strong. His light blue eyes were thickly lashed, and he had a neatly trimmed mustache. Good smile, too.

Inadvertently she noticed Lyon as he drifted into her peripheral vision. Well, maybe it wasn't all that inadvertent. He was hard to miss when he was standing, for he loomed above his employees. Even when he was sitting, his laughter carried to her, crisp and clear, over all other noises, a superb, atmospheric sound that made her heart leap.

His laugh rose again, rich and resonant in the warm air, and her heart reacted. Forcing her thoughts away from her host, she pretended nonchalance, taking a bite of pineapple. She swallowed with difficulty as the lawyer stopped beside the empty chair on her right. "May I join you?"

She looked up, remembering to sit back just a little, as though considering if she should allow him such a huge privilege. Counting to five, she gave him the smile Lyon taught her. "You don't look too dangerous," she teased softly.

"You mean for a lawyer?" He laughed, placed his plate on the table and sat. He was wearing a salmon-colored shirt over a matching swimsuit. The shirt was buttoned and she was glad. She wasn't ready for a bare chest at this close proximity just yet. She'd have to work up to that.

Belatedly, she remembered to smile at his little joke, shifting her legs away from his touch. She knew that was old Emily behavior, but she couldn't help it. "I'm afraid I don't recall your name," she lied. She knew coyness required that she not show great interest. Make him work for it.

He held out his hand, and she noticed his stubby fingers had well-groomed nails. "Wymon. Brice Wymon." They shook hands, and as she expected, his fingers squeezed and lingered. "And you're Emily, right?"

She smiled again, but removed her hand, taking up her glass of cola to sip. "Stone."

He adjusted his chair, and in doing so his hairy leg brushed hers. She sucked in a breath but forced herself to stay still, to endure the touch. When she did, she noticed that Brice pressed harder. Gritting her teeth, she managed to hold on to her smile. "So what do you do for Mr. Gallant, Brice?"

He shrugged, peeling a fat prawn and dipping it in a pool of shrimp sauce. "I'd rather talk about you, Emily. All I'm sure of is, you're a model."

He was sure of that? She toyed with her glass, wondering if she should bother with the truth. Everything else about this experience was bogus, and she knew she'd never see him after today. So why should she bore him with the mundane truth? She nodded. "You're so insightful, Brice," she cooed. Actually cooed! She was both horrified and a little impressed with herself. She didn't know she possessed a cooing gene.

He stuffed the prawn in his mouth and chewed, immediately taking up another. His leg, however, was pushing against hers so hard she was afraid if she didn't hold onto the chair he'd knock her off. "Are you kidding?" He went on munching. "What other kind of woman would Lyon have on his island but models and movie stars?"

She nodded, her jaws aching from her continued effort to smile flirtatiously. "Of course you're right," she agreed in her most syrupy tone.

A large shape emerged at her left and she glanced toward it, already aware that Lyon was coming their way. In an effort to appear utterly disinterested, she picked up her glass and lifted it to her lips. Unfortunately she couldn't manage to do more, for just at that moment his dark eyes met hers, and the effect was paralyzing. And there was no reason for it. His expression was merely polite, vaguely curious. When he reached the table, he paused. "Hello, Brice. Emily."

She put the cola glass down with a thud. He'd *never* called her by her given name before, and the sound of it spoken in his low-pitched voice set off a tingling all through her body.

"Great party, Lyon!" Brice lifted his drink in salute. "What I can't figure is how you always manage the greatest weather, too."

Lyon grinned. "Connections."

Emily pretended to admire the cut flowers, touching the soft petal of one golden lily.

"Are you enjoying yourself, Emily?" he asked.

Her breath caught again at the familiar use of her name. Knowing she couldn't simply pretend he wasn't there, she glanced his way, pasting on a smile. "Brice is so fascinating, I'd hardly noticed the party at all." *Oh, that was unkind!* She supposed her deep hurt had made her say it, and she was immediately sorry. Still, she didn't apologize.

His eyes narrowed a bit, not with anger but something else. Concern? Now that was crazy. Besides, she probably hadn't even seen the look at all, for he was grinning at Brice now. "I just wanted to say I've been informed the steaks will be ready in about ten minutes."

"Man, I'm ready," Brice enthused, plucking up another prawn and peeling it.

Emily gazed out to sea, wondering how Brice could stuff anything else down after all the food he'd consumed.

"Emily?" Lyon's coaxing tone was like the world's most powerful magnet, dragging her gaze to his face. When their eyes met, he merely nodded goodbye.

She nodded, too, stiffly, hating herself for caring. Dismissively, she shifted her perusal to Brice, gracing him with a brilliant show of teeth as he gobbled his last prawn.

Their conversation went smoothly throughout the steak course and the dessert course. Especially since she'd managed without much effort to get her dinner companion to talk about himself. So far she'd learned that he loved handball, loathed fishing, loved Stephen King—whoever he was—and planned to retire a millionaire at forty-five and play duplicate bridge for the rest of his life on some private beach just like this. She spent a lot of energy stifling yawns and working to keep herself from being tossed to the sand by Brice's constant leg butts. She began to fear she'd have a permanent dent where he kept jamming her with his shin.

As servants cleared away the remnants of dessert, cast-iron butterflies were doing real damage to her stomach. Operation Lay a Lawyer was rapidly approaching. Brice was definitely interested. He'd laughed and chatted, seeming to find her extremely good company, which was strange, since she hadn't opened her mouth except to eat for the past hour. Perhaps her smiling and nodding told him more than they seemed to—or, more likely, he was very superficial when it came to women. She supposed it was just as well that he didn't insist on knowing anything more about her than what he could see. She'd already lied about what she did for a living. She would only have had to continue to lie, something she wasn't very good at, anyway.

As the household staff took away tables and rearranged the chairs along the lawn's edge, the party turned into a beach dance. Emily stood beside Brice for a few minutes, watching Gallant employees and their spouses clutched together and swaying along the shore. Lyon was out there, of course, dancing with one of his female lawyers. She was a lovely brunette who could have been a model, too. Emily supposed she shouldn't be surprised that he would hire the most gorgeous female lawyers money could buy. She felt an unwelcome surge of envy for the woman clinging to him, smiling dreamily into his handsome face.

"Want to take a walk, Emily?"

She was startled to hear Brice's question— at least quite this soon. There was still an hour of light left. Somehow, she'd pictured their assignation in the darkness. Taking a heartening breath, she managed a smile. "I'd simply love to..." That was all she could steadily get out. Luckily, it sounded like a complete sentence. He grinned, tugging her away from the others. She chanced to see Meg, sitting between a couple of lawyers' wives. Meg was watching her and Brice with a sly smile on her face. When she knew Emily saw her, she gave her a discreet thumb's-up and winked.

Emily managed a frail smile that was really more of a resigned grimace, then turned toward her companion, determined to convince herself how good-looking and charming he was.

She knew this stretch of beach well. She'd jogged it every morning since the day in the cove when she'd tumbled over Lyon's toolbox. It was lovely along here. A band of chaste beach was sandwiched between the glistening skin of the sea and a dense palm and live oak woodland, which gave off a sultry perfume. The delicate chirps of the warblers greeted them as they walked, hand in hand, each thinking his own thoughts. She wondered if Brice's were as apprehensive as hers, but seriously doubted it.

Not far ahead, she recognized a little inlet that would be hidden from the rest of the party. Just thirty yards away. She wondered how many parties Brice had attended here, and if he already knew about the inlet—if he'd used it before like this. She closed her eyes. This was not productive thinking! She had to remember she was simply taking a class—a sexual class. She would get it behind her like evolution of amphibians, then move on with her life.

"You're a beautiful woman, Emily," Brice said, drawing her startled gaze. She smiled wearily. Of course he would say complimentary things. This was part of the seduction process.

"Thank you, Brice." Her breathlessness sounded more sexy than frightened, which she counted as a piece of luck. "You're—terribly attractive, yourself."

When they rounded the bend to the inlet, he indicated a secluded area of grasses amid masking ferns. "Why don't we sit down and enjoy the view."

She wanted to suggest the view had been fine where the party was going on but bit her tongue, nodding obligingly. She had to work on her nineties attitude. Maybe she should have had an alcoholic drink to lessen her inhibitions. But it was too late now. She'd have to do this cold sober. Stifling a sigh, she took a seat on the grass.

He sat down very close and faced her, his hip brushing against her thigh. His lime and coconut after-shave wafted around her, a scent she decided she could do without. Gamely she looked into his light eyes, unsettled to see lust glinting there. He leered at her, apparently misinterpreting her compliance as eagerness. "I've been lucky all my life." He scooted nearer. Now his left hip was rubbing her right. He leaned across her, planting a hand on the grass across her legs, his wrist against her thigh. She began to feel claustrophobic but tried to hide it as he went on, "But I can't believe my luck today." He leaned closer, his face only inches from hers.

Even though she was working at non-chalance, she tilted away from him. "What do you mean?"

He chuckled, running a finger up her arm, then along her collarbone. "You. I didn't think I'd have a chance with you. But here we are."

The iron butterflies in her stomach went berserk. "Where are we?"

He laughed. "I like that thing you do—that come-hither-*maybe* look. Really turns me on."

She smiled tremulously, ordering herself sternly not to chicken out this time. "Well, that always seems to work for me..." She winced, wondering where her brain was getting this stuff.

The finger on her collarbone turned into the palm of his hand. Applying pressure, he pushed her down on her back. She was so stunned by the haste of his action, she could only manage to stare wide-eyed. His lips came down on hers, heavy and mushy. Like dry marshmallows. His mustache scratched her upper lip. At the same time, the hand on her chest slipped down to cup her breast, kneading. He groaned, sliding over her.

She gasped, and his tongue took the opportunity to invade her mouth. The only urge she felt was to gag. Somehow, this wasn't working right. Oh, she knew her plan was to get the virgin part over, but she thought there would be more tenderness, more sharing. But Brice seemed to be of the notion that she was there to give and he to take—and take as quickly as possible.

Is this what it was like for Meg? Is this what she'd meant about the pickup and the gearshift scars? Emily supposed a woman's sexual initiation didn't have to be sparklers and firecrackers, but this was...

She dragged her face away, turning aside, and shoved hard at the hand squeezing her breast. *"Don't!"*

"Oh, baby..." He moaned greedily, ignoring her demand, evidently assuming it was her way of keeping the play-hard-to-get game going. His fingers crawled back, this time pushing her bathing suit strap down to give him better access to soft flesh. He moved farther over her to recapture her mouth, his tongue darting, poking.

She struggled, freeing her lips to plead, "Get *off*!" It was quivery and breathy, but loud enough for him to hear.

He chuckled. "Not on your life. Not after I spent all afternoon getting you here. We're through playing the tease game, so just relax and enjoy it."

He took hold of her other strap and yanked on them both. Stunned, she cried out, grabbing at her bodice for modesty. "Stop it! I've changed my mind." She was humiliated and hated herself. She knew Meg would be angry, but she couldn't go through with this. She'd thought the scene with Lyon on the kitchen table had made her feel dirty, but Brice was making her feel damaged. Like the victim of a crime.

"Come on, baby." He grunted, his lips nipping at her face, his mustache chafing her skin. "Enough's enough. It was cute at first, but now I'm getting ticked."

Grabbing her wrists, he forced her arms up on either side of her head, thrusting them into the grass. Though she shook her head from side to side, whimpering, he caught her mouth, savagely plunging his tongue inside. She wailed and kicked, but his legs were pinning hers, making her flailing worthless.

She grew terrified. He planned to go through with it against her will! She fought, clawing at his hands, but her efforts were futile. He was much too strong. When he transferred her left wrist over to hold both her arms with one beefy fist, she bounced her hips against his, kicked, cried out, knowing he was freeing up one hand to rip away her suit. She felt those neatly trimmed nails scrape along her shoulder as he jerked her strap down and knew she was helpless to stop him. They were too far away from the party for her cries to be heard over the band music and animated conversation. She lost hope. He was much too strong for her.

She squeezed her eyes shut, turning her face to the side. She might have to endure the violation, but she didn't want to suffer the memory of the viciousness that skulked in his eyes and twisted his mouth.

She heard a grunt, then a curse. Or was it the other way around? Without warning, Brice's weight was lifted away from her, as though he'd levitated himself straight up into the air. How or why that could happen didn't compute in her numbed mind. All she knew was that she was free of both his cruel restraints and his obscene weight.

Before she even opened her eyes, the impulse to flee took over, and she rolled away, scrambling toward the beach, sliding and skidding all the way to the edge of the water. When she felt roaming surf stroke her ankles, she gathered on her haunches, ready to run. Casting a panicked glance back to see if Brice was coming after her, she stilled, blinked, not sure to trust her eyes.

Lyon, not Brice, was loping her way, his expression stark, furious. She cowered on her hands, but before she could speak, he grasped her by her arms and lifted her to stand. "*Damn it*, Emily. Are you all right?"

She inhaled raggedly, dismayed by the thunder in his inquiry. Her emotions were already in tatters, and he was glowering at her, shouting at her. That's all she needed! Another irate man snarling in her face! She pushed against him. "Let go! Haven't I been manhandled enough for one day?"

The last came out in a sob, and it affected Lyon, changed his eyes, his expression. Suddenly he was holding her against his bare chest, and she could feel the reassuring drum of his heart. "I'm sorry," he whispered. "Are you all right?"

She relished the safe haven of his arms, the scent of him, his warm breath against her face, but she knew it was a fleeting haven. Pressing her palms against his chest, she shook her head. "Oh, Lyon..." His name on her lips seemed so right, another foolish notion she tried to shake off. "I'm okay, really. You can let go." When he didn't, she couldn't insist, chancing a look at his face. Remnants of anger lingered in his eyes. "Where's Brice?"

He flicked a glance over his shoulder, then looked at her, unsmiling. "He's napping."

She frowned, "Did you knock him out?"

"I'd rather say he's consciousness-challenged."

She felt terrible about what had happened, but she was more grateful that it was over than anything. Straining, she peered around Lyon's torso toward where she and Brice had struggled. Protruding from behind a wall of ferns was one lone foot. Very still. "Will he be okay?"

"Okay enough to stand in the unemployment line and face disbarment proceedings."

She shot her gaze to his grim face. "Oh, no, Lyon," she cried. "It—it was my fault."

His brows dipped at her assertion. Feeling deplorable guilt, she shoved against him but was too weak to be effective. "Let me go, Lyon," she cried, drained. She could feel his muscles flex as he held for another second before he released her and stepped away.

"You mustn't blame him," she mumbled, hating to have to make the admission.

"Really?" He didn't sound convinced. "So, you're saying you asked him to hold you down?"

She clutched one of her bruised wrists and rubbed, experiencing a surge of disgust. "No. Of course not!"

He nodded, pursing his lips. "But I gather you didn't say 'no' or 'stop' or 'don't'?"

She shivered uncontrollably, her glance veering out to sea. "Yes—yes, I told him to stop, but..."

"*Hell*, Emily. Did you ever tell me to stop?"

The gritted question came like a stunning blow. Of course, she had. She peeked sideways at him. She'd made him stop in exactly this situation, and he'd been a gentleman. He'd let her go—reluctantly, but he'd let her go. Nodding disjointedly, she lowered her glance to the sand, unable to speak.

"So, who's fault was it, then?"

He was right. Brice was a selfish, depraved piece of slime, and if Lyon hadn't come along, he would have *raped* her! Reality was starting to settle in, and she felt sick. Running trembling hands through her hair, she whispered brokenly, "I—I need to get his smell off me." As she headed into the surf, her sloshing became an uneven, unthinking flight. She thrashed and lurched into deeper and deeper water, desperate to get her attacker's stench off her skin. She knew she'd never smell lime and coconut again without feeling nauseated.

When the surging ocean was too deep for her to run anymore, she dove beneath the surface, grateful for the cooling rush of water against her flesh. As she came up, she gasped for air, pushing her hair from her eyes. Clearing her vision, she saw that Lyon was almost upon her. The sight of him there, oddly protective, his face drawn with worry, did something to her heart. Lightened it. She managed a brief smile. "I'm fine. Really. You can go back to your party."

He eyed her dubiously. "You're sure?"

She nodded. "I can take care of myself."

His lips twisted ruefully. "Well, you're welcome, sweetheart. Happy to help."

"Oh…" Her smile faded. His teasing made her grasp the truth—that she'd never thanked him for rescuing her. "How did you know to come?'' Her teeth chattered, and she hugged herself. She was strangely chilled, though the weather was quite warm.

He put out a hand. ''I think you're in shock, Emily. I'd better get you back. You might faint.''

''I'm not a fainter.''

''Try to keep that in mind.'' When she didn't take his hand, he grasped her fingers in his and drew her beside him. He startled her when he placed a supporting hand around her waist. ''If you start to feel light-headed, let me know.''

The irony of his suggestion was almost too much to deal with, and she had a crazy urge to laugh. Every time he touched her she grew light-headed, but she chose only to nod. ''And—thank you for what you did.''

He didn't reply as they returned to dry sand and he aimed her toward the party. ''Lyon?'' She balked. ''I can't go back there. I couldn't face people right now.''

He assayed her silently, then nodded, redirecting them through a wooded path toward the house. ''Rest. Around nine we're going to have a bonfire and roast hot dogs and marsh-mallows. You'll feel better then.''

She stared at him. ''Hot dogs? Really? I didn't think you knew about such ordinary activities.''

He grunted out a deep laugh. ''When I was a kid, dear old Dad shipped me off to spend summers with relatives in Texas. I was cheap labor and I ate a lot of hot dogs. Forgive me for bragging, but I know how to shovel manure, too.''

''A Renaissance man with cow poop on his Italian loafers.'' She found herself smiling. He'd never seemed more real, more accessible than at this moment. ''Actually, I've never been to a weenie roast,'' she admitted.

''Really?''

''Dad thought cooking on a stick was vulgar.''

He chuckled morosely. ''Apparently our fathers were a lot alike.''

''A week ago, I would never have guessed we had anything in common,'' she mused. A thought struck, and she remembered the question he'd sidestepped earlier. ''By the way, Lyon, how did you happen to show up just in time?''

He shrugged. She could feel it in the tightening of his hand at her waist. ''You weren't fooling me with that coy-kitten act at the table. I knew what you were planning, and I had a bad feeling about Brice.'' Reproof glittered in his eyes. ''You'd have been better off with Kevin.''

With his observation, she felt a niggle of disappointment somewhere deep inside. More than a niggle. It was a flood of disappointment that turned quickly into an ocean of gloom. For a few crazy minutes she'd allowed herself to float around in a fantasy land where Lyon Gallant actually cared about *her*! Oh, he knew how to act like a gentleman with a woman, all right. But he'd just made it very clear—*again*—that he didn't know how to love one. Didn't have any desire to try.

How silly she'd been to personalize his rescue. He'd just engaged in a little analyzing, putting two and two together and coming up with a four that might put a damper on his expensive party. He didn't care if she lost her virginity, or to whom. She just needed to *select* better!

Gouging her fingers beneath his, she wrenched his hand from around her waist. In a desperate rush, she stepped out of his sensual aura. "I tell you what, Lyon, *sweetheart*! Why don't you make up a list of suitable candidates for the job." She whirled to glare at him, her body quaking with fury. He was staring at her, appearing confused— the self-centered, know-it-all man that he was! How dare he have the gall to be confused!

"Or better yet, why don't you be a good little host and pick out somebody you think would 'do me' with a minimum of muss and fuss and send him to my room!"

She whirled away. Unable to look at him any longer, she sprinted unsteadily toward the mansion—away from dreams she'd begun to spin during the flash of insanity she'd experienced within his sheltering embrace.

CHAPTER NINE

IT WAS after midnight, and Emily watched as the bonfire dwindled and the scent of roasted hot dogs faded along with the voices. Apparently, the party was finally over. She hated herself for skulking on her balcony like a pouty child, wishing she was out there with him—er, *them*. She'd always imagined a weenie roast as a lighthearted thing to do. As a child she'd never really played as other children did because her father had disapproved of frivolous noise. Lyon's invitation to join the party had been hard to resist, but she was too torn up by his indifferent attitude about women and sex to bear being near him.

Still, she wondered if the partygoers had sharpened sticks to poke their hot dogs and marshmallows on, like she'd seen on the Boy Scout special on TV, or if they'd used silver skewers. Probably the skewers, considering the opulence of Lyon's life-style. She exhaled heavily. Being the coward she was, she would

237

never know for sure. But even from where she watched on her balcony, she did know the cool evening breeze, the scent of fire and cooking food, the laughter mingling with the soft music and whispering surf, seemed terribly carefree and idyllic. Probably the very reason people went off to tropical islands in the first place. For just that sort of back-to-nature, barefoot way of living. Unhappy, she turned away from the rail, half wishing she'd followed her instincts and rejoined the party—at least long enough to taste a roasted weenie. She could have avoided Lyon for fifteen minutes, couldn't she?

Not only that, Brice was long gone. She'd heard the distant thwap-thwap-thwap of the helicopter and the howl of its engine a couple of hours ago. There was no question her attacker had been ejected from both the party and the island by Gallant security people. At least she didn't have to worry about him any longer. But what of other men like him? Evidently she wasn't much of a judge. Harry had been a cheat, Lyon a heartless playboy and now Brice an amoral brute.

She walked inside her room, deciding it was absurd that she'd gotten dressed in shorts and a blouse just to pace the floor and feel sorry for herself. It would have been more sensible if she'd put on her nightgown and gone to bed. Why had she held onto the hope that Lyon would come up and insist she come back to the party?

The knock at her door made her stumble to a halt and set her heart hammering. Could it possibly be? Silly, girlish optimism surged in spite of everything. "Who—who's there?"

The knock sounded again, and she realized her response had been too frail to be heard. She scurried to the door. "Who is it?"

"Miss Stone?"

She leaned against the wood, dejected. The man's voice wasn't Lyon's. "Yes?"

"Mr. Gallant sent me."

She frowned at the cream-colored panels. "He did?"

"Yes. I'm sorry, I'm a little late."

His discretionary tone confused her for a second, then the implication slammed into her brain like a truck. She took an involuntary step backward, shocked. Okay, so she'd dared

Lyon to send her a man. But she was sure he knew she'd been angry and was just spouting off. She hadn't actually meant it. "I—I don't need anything," she insisted in a strained voice.

"I'm sorry, Miss Stone. Mr. Gallant told me you might try to send me away. But he said I should be insistent—for your own good."

Her jaw dropped. "For my own *good*?" Incredulous, she scowled at the door. "Look, I know why you're here and I'm appalled that you would go along with such a scummy idea." She flung the door wide to glare her distaste at him. The young man was certainly impressive looking, in his white slacks and shirt, the Gallant's distinctive script G embroidered in gold over his heart. His hair was blond and just curly enough to be boyishly appealing. His eyes were light green and big, his lips as pretty as any movie hunk's. She glowered at him, her fists balled. "Well, at least you're *handsome*."

The young gigolo blinked, but otherwise maintained his aplomb. "Thank you, Miss Stone."

"However, I'm not—and I repeat *not*—having sex with you, no matter what Mr. Gallant insists!"

The man's eyes widened, and his lips parted in what could only have been astonishment. "Ma'am?" Though he'd spoken quietly, Emily could detect alarm in his voice.

She began to smell a very big rat. Something was wrong here. This husky, hired sex partner didn't seem to be aware of his carnal mission. "Mr. Gallant did send you here to—to..." A clammy chill settled over her. She couldn't say *that* word again. As she fumbled for a less explicit way of asking the same question, the man's face turned crimson all the way to his ears. Feeling a blush heat her own cheeks, she demanded, "Then why did he send you here?"

His Adam's apple worked as he took a step sideways, indicating a rolling tray that had been hidden by his brawny torso. What she saw made her face burn in earnest. It was a covered silver tray. And she had a sickening feeling it didn't contain kinky sex toys.

"Your dinner, ma'am." The answer held a cautious edge, and her heart went out to the

poor guy. Clearly he was disconcerted by what
he had to assume was sex games of the rich
and famous.

She was horrified at herself, and embarrassed beyond words for her assumption
about why he'd been sent to her room. But
the miserable waiter's expression was so
priceless, she couldn't restrain a choked
giggle. "Food?" She gulped down another
nervous laugh. "You brought *food*?"

He nodded, his features distrustful, as
though he expected her to become sexually
frustrated and start ripping at his clothes. It
seemed she wasn't a total femme fatale, after
all. This poor young employee didn't appear
overwhelmed by her charms. He looked more
panicked than anything. Rubbing her temples,
she grimaced apologetically. "I'm sorry. I'm
not hungry." Indicating the tray, she waved it
away. "Please take it back."

Even as embarrassed as she was, and facing
the waiter's total chagrin, she felt a growing
animosity for a certain mischievous host. Did
Lyon have any idea when he'd sent this good-
looking waiter to her that she would get the

wrong idea? Did he mean for her to be humiliated?

"I—I'll just be going, then," the man mumbled, grasping the tray. Apparently, in the face of her obvious sexual dementia, he'd decided to forget his orders about being insistent.

"Please, tell Mr. Gallant..." She paused, not sure how much she wanted to say. He looked back, anxiety flashing across his face again. If Lyon had done this with malice aforethought, he'd been unkind to this shy young waiter—possibly scarred him for life about ever handling room service again. "Just tell Mr. Gallant he owes you a raise."

Looking uncomfortable, he nodded obligingly. "Yes, ma'am." He left as quickly as the cart would allow, and she didn't blame him for his shuffling escape. She wondered how long it would take for this story to get around, and was thankful she'd be leaving in a few days.

Once inside her room, she slumped against the door and started to laugh. She laughed so hard, tears came to her eyes. Then she began to sob.

* * *

Sleep was out of the question. Strangling Lyon Gallant seemed like a productive idea, but then, there were annoying laws about such things. So, as a compromise, she decided she had to roam. Even the huge mansion proved too confining, so very quickly she found herself outside, walking along the sand, inhaling the ocean breeze, hoping the tranquillity of the night would calm her spirits.

Her mind leaped around, not settling on any one thought. The reason, she knew, was that her mind wanted so badly to settle on Lyon Gallant, and she couldn't allow that. So it was with total surprise that she found herself at the cove. She hadn't gone there on purpose. She would *never* have gone there on purpose. But clearly, some baser part of her subconscious had needed to seek out the spot for its own demented reasons.

She looked around the moonlit bay, then at the skeletal cabin. All was still but for the rustling of leaves in the trade winds and the soft hushing sound of the water gliding along the sand. She was alone in the moon-washed quiet. At least she assumed she was alone. She remembered the last time she'd wandered here. Believing she was by herself, she'd stumbled on her host—naked. Deciding it was better to be safe, she called, ''Hello?''

Nothing answered her but the ocean and the breeze.

''Lyon, if you're lurking around here naked, please tell me.''

Still only nature's night voices called to her, soft and welcoming. She was truly alone this time. Relieved, she scanned the dark waters in the cove. Bright ripples winked in the moonlight. Her mind tumbled to when she'd thought she'd acted so uncivilized by rolling up her shorts and wading into this same cove. That recollection made her smile. How naive she'd been. Had it been just over three weeks ago? It seemed like a lifetime. Today, she wouldn't even think twice about rolling up her shorts. Not only that, she would have no compunction at all about taking off her shoes. She couldn't even do that the last time she'd waded here.

Feeling a sudden urge, she sat on the grass at the edge of the sand and slipped off her tennis shoes and then her socks. Laying them aside, she glanced at the inviting waters, then frowned as another, more daring idea struck. Why not, she decided, tugging her T-shirt off over her head, then unfastening her bra. Standing, she slipped out of her shorts and panties. She felt like swimming nude. *And she would!*

She was excited by her new found spontaneity, though she still folded her clothes before venturing into the water. That dichotomy in her character made her laugh out loud. Emily Stone—the methodical wild woman. She giggled again, wading in until the sea lapped at her hips. Diving under, she felt amazingly free, like some native in a primitive land. It was liberating, and she came up laughing.

Floating on her back, she kicked her feet and gazed at the man in the moon. Even though he leered at her, she felt no embarrassment. She was discovering things about herself. She was a perfectly worthy person, and for the first time in her life, she felt like she was just exactly *fine*. She was as competent a teacher as her father had been, and she was as desirable a woman as Elsa.

She had old-fashioned morals, yes, but she decided that wasn't so bad. Surely someday, some man would come along who wasn't a cheat or a degenerate or a self-centered egotist, and that man would find her perfect, old-fashioned morals and all.

Her thoughts sobered and her smile left her face. She hoped that would happen, at least. She wanted to share her life with a nice man. She stopped kicking and let her legs sink to the sand. Standing up, she was surprised how deep the water was. Enjoying the caress of the cool foam across her breasts, she pushed curls out of her eyes. She'd gone out pretty far and decided she'd better start back. If she got caught in a tide heading away from land, she'd be in serious trouble.

When she turned toward shore, she stilled. Lyon was standing there, all moonlit and splendid, his legs braced wide, his arms crossed over his bare chest. He was wearing shorts and nothing else. Apparently he could tell the second she spotted him, for his hands went to his hips and he inclined his head toward the sand. "Whose clothes are these, Miss Stone?" he called across the distance.

She bit her lip. Now she knew why the moon had been leering at her. He'd known

Lyon was watching and found her predicament extremely comical. Drat all male
species—be they human or jeering extrater-
restrial rocks!

"Are these your clothes?" he asked,
bending down. When he came up, her bra
dangled from his finger. "Very serviceable,"
he commented dryly.

She blanched. "Put that down and keep
your opinions to yourself!" Though she was
in deep water, she reflexively covered her
breasts. "Why aren't you in bed with that
pretty lawyer?"

He chuckled, dropping the underwear on
her other clothing. "Haven't you heard how
bad workplace affairs can be?"

She pushed a hand through curls that had
blown over her eyes, not pleased with his
taunting. As if he cared about the rules of
sexual conduct! "I don't know what you
mean," she retorted sarcastically. "I have affairs at school all the time! Teachers, students—"

"Sweetheart, if anybody knows that's bull,
I do."

The reference to her lack of sexual experience reminded her of why she'd come out here in the first place, and she shot back, "Enough about me. Let's talk about that little trick you played tonight! That was really mean."

Though her eyes were accustomed to the dark, and the moon glow made his body look disturbingly virile, she couldn't quite see his expression from this distance. Still, she had a feeling one of his brows rose in question. "Trick?"

She laughed disparagingly. "Oh, that's priceless. Don't deny you sent that man to my room *knowing* I'd think he planned to have sex with me. That was low!"

Emily watched him closely in the quiet, trying to guess his expression. Was he amused? Confused? Angry?

"You thought I sent Jeffery up there to embarrass you?"

She didn't like the slither of discomfort that shot through her at his skeptical tone. "Oh, don't act like it never occurred to you."

She thought she saw a brief flash of teeth. "Hell, Emily, I told him to take you a hot dog, since you'd never had one. Jeffery's the son of my security chief, and he's going to start studying for the priesthood next fall. You probably scared him to death.''

Her stomach knotted. Why did she suddenly feel like she was the only one having carnal thoughts around here? ''I don't believe you!'' she said desperately, hoping he was lying but afraid he wasn't.

''Emily—''

''And don't call me that!'' She was so upset, she was lashing out at anything and everything. She knew it, but couldn't help herself.

''I thought Emily was your name.''

''Not to *you*!''

''Okay—Miss Stone. How's the water?''

Suffering at being caught in such a demoralizing situation, she couldn't stand to see him remain so calm and in control. Refusing to allow him to stand there making idle conversation, she challenged defensively, ''How long have you been spying on me?''

''Spying?''

She had a dreadful thought and glared dubiously at him. "Were you lurking around in the dark when I called out to you?"

He pursed his lips but said nothing. She couldn't tell if he was surprised by the question and had no idea what she was talking about, or just keeping her in suspense. Anxious, she shouted, "I suppose you didn't feel you had to answer because I asked if you were naked, and you were in a swimsuit. It was a perfect loophole. Don't lie!"

"I wouldn't think of it."

She stiffened with indignation at his evasion. Had he seen her nude or hadn't he? "What's the use! You'll tell me whatever you want to, anyway," she muttered, shaking her head.

"What?" he called. "I didn't quite hear you."

She glowered at him, shouting, "I said, I hope you enjoyed yourself!"

"I always try to, sweetheart."

She huffed with frustration. This was getting her nowhere. "So what are your plans now? Setting up a video camera?"

His crooked grin was clear in the moonlight, and she trembled in reaction. "Actually, I'd planned on swimming."

Her worst fears seemed confirmed, but she had to ask. "Naked?"

He lifted a nonchalant shoulder, his teeth continuing to gleam in the moon's radiance. "You say it as though you're shocked by the idea." He ambled a few steps forward. "That's pretty hypocritical, wouldn't you say? Considering where your clothes are."

"But..." She clamped her jaws tight, with no idea how to answer that. He was right, of course. "But I'm *alone*! I planned to *stay* alone," was all she could come up with.

"Me, too." He hooked a threatening thumb beneath his waistband. "Funny how things work out."

"Don't you dare!"

He didn't go further with the action. Just eyed her for a long moment. "It's my cove. Remember?"

"You could go away—for a few minutes!"

"Oh?" He removed his thumb, his tone ripe with amusement. "And why would I do that?"

"Because—maybe—you're a gentleman?"

He chuckled. "That sounds like you're guessing. Don't you know by now?"

"You spy on me in the dark, and you have the gall to ask me that?"

A silver slash of moonlight highlighted his brows as they furrowed. "Look, Miss Stone. The first rule of swimming in the ocean is not to go out alone. You're no longer in the protected cove. And if you'll pardon an observation, you're only a fair swimmer. Gentleman or no gentleman, it's my duty to make sure you're okay."

"Well, I'm *fine*," she shouted, abashed. Could he honestly have been concerned for her safety? The probability seemed so remote it was almost laughable—almost. "Well—if that's *really* the case, feel free to quit playing lifeguard and go."

"Not until I know you're safely out."

She heaved a moan that held an obscene undertone. "Then we'll both be here forever, because I'm not marching out naked in front of you, no matter what you might have already seen!"

"Maybe I could turn around."

"Maybe you could go to blazes, too!"

"You're in a bad mood, sweetheart," he said. "I don't think I've seen this side of you before."

"And you probably think it's the current economic downturn that has me upset— you'll blame anything but *yourself*!"

He was silent for a minute, all moonlit, lean-limbed muscle. She stared, unable to help herself. The man was physically impeccable yet emotionally inaccessible. "I got here five minutes ago," he finally said, and for some crazy reason she believed him. With a shrug, he added, "I'll wait for you over the ridge, but you have to keep talking so I'll know you're okay."

She frowned in confusion. "Talking?"

"Or you could sing."

She shook her head with exasperation. "Go. I'll talk."

"What about?"

He was being downright difficult, and he knew it. "I'll discuss how much I *hate* you. That should take awhile."

"This could be enlightening." Presenting her with his impressive back, he started to walk away. "Okay. I'm listening."

She watched him head up the slope. He even walked sexy. She shoved the unruly thought from her mind. "First of all, you think you're right all the time," she shouted. "Which you're not!" He kept moving, reaching the crest of the hill, then started down the other side. "And you're way too addicted to making money. There's more to life than money and possessions and—and *toys*, you know!"

He'd descended to where she could only see him from the waist up, then just from the shoulders. "I don't like the way you—you go without socks!" She was grasping at straws. In all honesty, there was very little she didn't like about him. The only thing that really got to her was his inability, or unwillingness, to see women as equals, as possible life partners.

"And—and I don't like the way you—the way you *kiss*!" She was lying now. It was a huge, bold-faced fabrication that tasted like ash on her tongue.

He'd dropped out of sight, so she decided she'd better make fast work of getting out of the water and throwing on her clothes. "You're the type of man every girl is warned about by her mother," she yelled. "You're Mr. Soft-Talking Hard-Hearted Virgin Hunter who leaves women broken in the dust at your feet. And you don't even notice!"

She lurched to shore and began hurriedly throwing on her T-shirt and shorts. "You yourself admitted you think of women as toys. Well, let me tell you, Mr. Gallant, you're missing out on the important things in life with your male chauvinist thinking. Did you know that men who live the longest are married? And men who live the fewest years are bachelors?"

She stuffed her bra into the end of a tennis shoe along with her socks, deciding she didn't need to put everything on. The quicker she got away from him, the better. In the darkness, he'd never notice she wasn't wearing her bra, anyway. Hiking up the slope, she added loudly, "I'm sure you think it's better to live a short, wild life than a long contented one, so there's no use arguing with you about

it. To be frank, I could care less if you ever
get married, because as far as I'm concerned
you're the last person on earth I'd want to
marry!'' When she reached the top of the rise,
she could see him. He was lounging on the
beach, leaning against a crooked palm tree.
His legs were outstretched before him, crossed
at the ankles, and he was staring out to sea.
When she stopped speaking, he looked her
way, unsmiling.

"Is that all you hate about me?" he queried
thinly.

She lifted her chin in defiance. Had she
pricked his ego? *Good!* If anybody in the
world needed his ego pricked, Lyon Gallant
did. "That's enough reasons for now," she
said, reluctantly continuing in his direction.
"You can go get naked if you want. I'll find
my own way back."

He stood. "I've lost my desire to swim."
When he spoke, she had just reached him.
Intent on sweeping disdainfully by, she was
stunned to find herself dragged into his arms.
His lips came down hard on hers, taking away
her breath and sapping her of any fight she
might have put up if she'd had an inkling this

was about to happen. She heard her tennis shoes thud to the sand, but her mind was far from concerned about such trivial details.

He crushed her to him, shattering her with the thrilling hunger of his kiss. Her stomach swirled wildly, and her arms lifted to encircle his broad torso, though she berated them for their treachery. His softly furred chest was like heaven against her breasts, and when she heard his low moan, she sensed he was aware that only a scrap of damp fabric separated them from blissful, intimate contact.

The raw passion in Lyon's touch was dazzling as his hands massaged, stroked, titillated. Quickly, she became aware that she wasn't the only one affected. They were too closely bound together for her to miss the increased thud of his heart or the pulsing heat of his arousal.

She knew he was angry, yet his lips were velvet and warm against hers. His hands scorched sensual trails of possession down her back, breathtaking punishment for her great, horrible lie about his kisses being flawed. He meant to prove her a liar, and she was powerless to defend herself against his ploy.

She could only sag into his welcome hardness, clutching, kissing him back with all her womanly strength and helpless love.

He released her suddenly, backing away. She swayed but managed not to sink to her knees. Feeling chilled and alone, she tried to catch her breath. She couldn't speak, couldn't form a thought. Her mind was a blur, her empty arms aching with longing.

"You have a strange way of showing hatred, sweetheart," he muttered huskily, his features grim. She'd expected to see triumph in his expression, but she saw only anger there.

It seemed as though he was about to say something else, but he bit it off. Instead, he jerked a hand through his hair, gritting out a curse. "I think I need that swim, after all."

He was gone before she could move.

CHAPTER TEN

IT HAD been raining off and on all day, the atmosphere as dismal as Emily's soul. Gloom squeezed at her heart, causing intolerable pain. She didn't know if Lyon was on the island or not, and wished she didn't care. A sense of fury and loss bore down on her and she moaned in anguish. *Oh, how could I have allowed myself to fall so hopelessly in love with a man who doesn't believe such a soft emotion exists?*

Her sad query was swallowed by the bark of thunder. Windows rattled, proof that a storm was building. Meg's cheerful personality would have been a welcome diversion, but she and Ivy were once again immersed in a hot game of chess.

Emily didn't have the heart to intrude on their last evening together, so she worked at keeping her mind off Lyon by trying to read, then attempting to sleep. Neither worked. She paced, watched the rain and avoided looking at herself in the mirror, hating the heartbreak in her eyes.

Desperate and miserable, she found herself opening the drawer that held the Gallant's underwear Meg had insisted on purchasing for her several weeks ago. Wondering what malicious creature had taken over her brain, she stared at the lacy bra and panties as she carried them across her room and laid them out on her bed.

Considering Meg's unblushing taste, her purchase for Emily had been wildly conservative. Though the bra was skimpy, it was fashioned of eyelet lace, lending it a charming, country-girl feel, rather than making it seem like something a stripper might wear. The panties were a bikini cut, also of pink eyelet. Somehow, the scanty garment seemed more sweet than lewd, yet sexy in a chaste way. She had to give Meg credit. If Emily were ever to wear anything from a *Gallant's* catalogue, it well might be this.

But she *wouldn't*, she insisted, lifting the bra to look at it closely. She had promised herself she wouldn't try to compete in *his* arena. She wouldn't wear the type of clothes *his* women wore. She didn't want to be just another in a long line of Lyon Gallant's conquests.

Yet even as she swore to herself that she would never try on the bra and panties, she was slipping out of her own underwear. A moment later she found herself staring in the mirror at someone who looked very much like Emily Stone—but this unknown woman was clad in scraps of pink eyelet.

The racy bra was a plunging style with a cleavage-enhancing shape. She stared open-mouthed. "My goodness," she breathed in astonishment, not recognizing her boosted figure. The panty legs were cut high on her hips while the waistband didn't even pretend to reach her waist, hugging her anatomy well below the navel. And the back of the panties—well, it was all but nonexistent. She bit her lower lip. What had possessed her to put these on? Just how weak was she, giving in to her urge to see herself the way Lyon judged all women?

More thunder boomed, and a windswept branch thudded against the panes of her patio door, though Emily hardly noticed. In an odd trance, she made a slow turn, stifling a gasp when she saw her bare bottom come into view. Closing her eyes, she vowed this lapse would be her guilty secret, and hers alone. Even Meg would never know she'd succumbed to such an indiscreet impulse.

An explosion shattered the window. Emily threw up her arms to protect her face, cowering away from the unknown cataclysm. What was it? Hurricane-force winds ripping away the wall? A crashing helicopter? She felt the cold bite of rain soak her bare skin and hair, the harsh gale knocking her backward. Stumbling, her survival instincts took over. She lunged out of her room, slamming into another obstruction, and cried out in panic. *The whole place was collapsing!*

"Good God, Emily!" came a rough voice. At the same instant her flight was halted as strong, steadying arms held her close. "Are you hurt?"

Her mind had been working so fast in an effort to come through whatever holocaust had befallen the mansion, it only took a split second to realize she'd hurtled herself into Lyon's massive form. Relieved, she sagged against him, her arms going around his chest in a stranglehold. "Oh, Lyon," she cried. "What—what happened?"

"I don't know. It looks like a tree fell." He paused, and she could tell he was examining the damage from his vantage point outside her room. "I was coming to tell you to move to a lower level during the high winds."

She swallowed, lifting her face to look into his. "Oh." Her heart hammered as she saw the worry on his handsome features, and she feared the blind dread that had choked her only seconds before had turned into bleak, helpless adoration. She had to get control of her emotions, distance herself from him. Snaking her arms from about his torso, she placed trembling hands against his chest. "I'm..." Her voice sounded like sandpaper on rough wood, and she cleared her throat. "I'm fine. Just wet." With great effort, she managed a brave smile.

His expression didn't ease, and blissful eons passed as he held her close. His gaze moved over her face, his eyes narrowed, contemplative.

"Lyon?" she repeated. "Please..."

The entreaty in her voice seemed to shake him from his lassitude, and he released her. As his glance raked her nearly nude form, one elegant brow winged upward. "Well," he murmured. "I approve."

His comment reminded Emily of how she was dressed—or *undressed.* "Oh, my heavens." Disgraced, she covered herself as well as she could, positive this would go into her diary as her worst living moment!

With a smile twitching at the corners of his mouth, Lyon began to unbutton his dress shirt. Though every fiber of her being was shouting at her to run, she could only tremble, watching him disrobe with an economy of motion that was lithe and thrillingly male. Her admiring gaze traveled along the play of muscle across his chest as he shrugged out of his shirtsleeves. She was insane, lost in her love for him. What was he going to do? Did it matter anymore? Could she stop him even if she wanted to?

The warmth of expensive cotton came around her like his very arms, like love itself. If only it had been his love, rather than his cast-off shirt. The fabric clung to her, sopping up the dampness of the storm, taking away the chill.

Lyon's hand engulfed hers, and he led her away from the windy doorway to the staircase.

"Where are we going?"

"Out of the wind." He headed down the steps with her in tow.

She tugged on his hold. "Not your apartment." It wasn't a question.

He stopped and looked at her. As they were standing, with Lyon several steps below her, they were eye to eye. He studied the stubborn, frightened set of her features, his gaze burning as it roved. "Emily…" He took a step toward her. When she retreated, he halted, mouthing a curse. "You stand there all damp and flushed, reluctantly desirable, with *my* shirt clinging to your body where *my* hands should be," he growled with soft menace. "Dammit, you should be on the cover of *Gallant's* looking just that way—and you should be in my bed—*tonight*."

She stared, stunned by the raw vehemence in his voice. Every nerve in her body hummed, every muscle tensed. She wanted him but couldn't risk reaching out, touching his bunching jaw. Yet her hand tingled with the need to feel him, hold him.

She knew if she did, he would get his way—his conquest—and she would never wholly mend from the encounter. How dare he do this to her? He was well aware of his sensual power—this womanizing scoundrel bent on victory—and she was nothing more to him than a *toy*!

She lifted a rebellious chin. "Aren't you kind to offer me a few spare minutes of your time." Her voice was weak but dripped with sarcasm. "However, I don't need your love lessons. I'm fine the way I am. Someday, some man will come along who will care for *me*—pesky morals and all."

He frowned, chagrin flickering across his face. "Do you realize no woman before you has ever turned me down?" His voice was low, raw. He clutched her hand as though he couldn't comprehend her rejection, expecting her to follow him anywhere, no matter what.

She smiled, then giggled. It was a hysterical reaction, but she couldn't help it. "Don't worry, *sweetheart*. You're still irresistible. Why do you think I put on this—this damnable underwear?'' she blurted, tears rushing to her eyes. ''Because I wanted to—just for a minute—see if I could compete with *your* women!'' She bit her tongue, hating herself for admitting that. Hating herself for giving him ammunition. But she knew she was stronger now. She could resist the temptation of a wild, last-minute fling. There was too much to lose if she gave in. So if Lyon tried to take her tonight, she would fight him, and it would be worse than any violation Brice had intended on the beach.

His expression remained disbelieving and hard, and the sensual heat that crackled between them grew almost tangible. She could tell her stern assertion nettled him, and that he was fighting to control himself. As their staring battle raged, she saw something new flash in his eyes and had the oddest sense it was helplessness. He didn't know how to handle unconditional rejection. Mr. Know It All Sex God had never had to before! Stormy seconds passed before his lips finally lifted in a grim smile. ''You've learned one thing from our association, at least.''

She blanched. "What do you think I've learned?"

"That being ravishing and sexy has its down side. I'd suggest you take self-defense classes when you get back to Iowa. Or at least learn to keep your clothes on in public."

Her sharp intake of breath signaled her offense, and she yanked herself from his hold. "I liked you better when you were nothing more than a conceited handyman!" A thought hit her and she demanded, "Why are you building that cabin, anyway?"

From the abrupt furrowing of his brow, she could tell he was taken off guard by her question. It was almost as though that thought had occurred to him, too. "It's a hobby," he muttered. The uncharacteristic distraction and vulnerability in his eyes were so seductive she felt an unwelcome rush of caring for him.

He must have sensed her wavering, for before she could react, she was in his arms, his lips playing softly across hers, delighting, tempting, wearing down her resistance.

His hands were heady fire along her skin, the damp fabric heating under his touch. His fingers lingered here, tormented there, roved downward to slip beneath his shirt to cup her bare backside. She moaned, but her arms betrayed her, clutching the welcome, naked flesh of his shoulders. More than life, more than self-respect, she relished the tensing of muscle as he drew her into his hard body.

She was swept up into his arms, their lips and tongues dancing together with joyous abandon. Her brain caught on the fact that she was being whisked down the stairs. She had no idea how he could kiss her and move so swiftly along a precarious surface. But here she was sailing down flight after flight, being expertly kissed all the while.

After an interminable period of quandary as to how he was managing such a feat, she faced the truth. *She* was the one clinging to his lips, her arms wound tightly around his neck, her fingers woven in his hair. She had a niggling suspicion and opened one eye, suddenly finding herself staring into his dark gaze.

Pulling away, she objected, "Your eyes aren't closed!"

He grinned. "Somebody had to navigate, sweetheart."

The silver sparkle of triumph in his eyes gave her a jolt. She was within a hair's breadth of total surrender, and he was delighted with the knowledge. And why shouldn't he be? His seduction record was about to go unbroken. Emily shuddered with shame. After all her mental warring on the subject. After telling him outright that she *didn't* intend to be another of his conquests. Here she was, in his arms, panting and whimpering with desire, on the way to his *bed*!

More angry with herself than she'd evei been, she wriggled violently, shoving against his shoulders. "Let me down! I've learned my lesson!"

It was no surprise that he didn't drop her like a hot poker. She was still struggling in his arms when he asked, "What lesson?"

"I'll slap your face if you don't drop me this instant!"

"You don't really want that."

His eyes were beguiling, full of such stirring beauty a less determined woman would have melted with need. Knowing she was teetering on the brink of disaster, she swung out rashly, hitting his cheek with all the anger and frustration inside her. She glared at him, her hand throbbing, daring him wordlessly not to do as she'd demanded.

He blinked, startled that she'd actually slapped him. His lips twisted cynically. "Apparently you meant that." He lowered her to her feet but didn't step away, leaving her to flounder on passion-weakened limbs.

Coming up against a wall, she leaned into it, glowering at him. She was all set to unleash her rage, but halted just as her lips parted, captured by his arresting presence. Even now, after she'd promised herself to despise him, now, when he was obviously angry, charisma radiated from him, intimidating and paralyzing her.

Thank heaven he didn't come near, or her wits would have flown away like so many frightened fireflies and she would have run into his arms. "What lesson?" he repeated darkly.

She willed her pulse to slow, though his scent clung to her as surely as his shirt did, and her lips throbbed with the heat of his kisses. Her world reeled, and to sustain herself she willed her eyes shut to block out the stimulating vision of him. ''I—I've learned that making love with someone who doesn't care about you makes you feel hollow, empty,'' she cried. ''I don't want to feel that way.''

After an eternity of uneasy silence, she couldn't help but look at him, once again thrown off-center by his virile good looks. His jaw was clenched, his eyes hooded and impenetrable. Forcing herself to speak, she admonished him, ''I believe you feel empty all the time—except maybe when you're working on your cabin.''

For an instant he looked as though he'd been slapped again, but quickly his teeth flashed in a twisted grin. ''What do I owe you for that psychoanalysis?''

Her heart shuddered to a stop, and she couldn't keep a mewling sound of defeat from escaping her throat. Shattered, she spun away and ran, unwilling to have him witness her desolate tears.

The next time she saw him was in the morning. He was standing near the patio, beside a garden area filled with gardenia bushes heavy with fragrant flowers. Another photo shoot was about to begin, and a bevy of leggy models were gathered around him, all plainly enamored, all practically naked. Emily pressed forward across the lawn, forcing her gaze not to veer from the helicopter that awaited her, ready to transport her and Meg to Miami for their return flight home.

Lyon's rich laughter rang out over the feminine giggles, and without realizing it, she shifted to stare in his direction. His glance caught hers and cruelly held it, his grin fading only slightly. The captivity lasted two or three seconds before one of the models slipped her arm through his, drawing his glance and releasing Emily once again to breathe, to move, to get on with her life.

She jerked back, numbly accepting a hug from Ivy and trying valiantly to listen to Meg's chatter. Inside the helicopter, she leaned against the plush leather seat and clutched at her throat, feeling sick. All she could see in her mind's eye was a dark, hypnotic gaze—a gaze that seemed to hold both fury and tenderness in the same unfathomable glance. How could that be? It suddenly came to her that Lyon Gallant had come to care for her—at least a little—and *hated* her for it.

As they lifted away from the earth, she closed her eyes, pondering how she would ever manage to erase that painful discovery from her heart.

CHAPTER ELEVEN

EMILY tried to be excited about the first day of school. She always had been before. But after leaving Sin Island seven weeks ago, a pall had settled over her heart, letting very little contentment in. She'd compelled herself to think positively, and she'd actually made changes in her life. Both little and big. But nothing she tried could dim her foolish longing for Lyon Gallant.

As she rushed along the high school campus sidewalk toward the 1930s era brick building, she could feel the eyes of her students on her and had to smile inwardly. She supposed she did look different in her trim, tailored suit with the nipped-in waist and short skirt. She had a feeling the senior boys nudging each other nearby hadn't been aware she even owned a pair of knees before today.

Turning toward the main entrance, she had a misstep when she realized Harry was standing at the bottom of the wide fan of stairs. She inhaled for strength. The man was a glutton for punishment. Clamping her jaws together, she marched toward him. He was beaming at her, but she could see the nervous twitch he always had in his left eye when he was anxious.

He waved a bouquet of yellow roses. "Hi, Em."

She came up before him and smiled tiredly. "Hello, Harry. Isn't this out of your way?"

His pale features colored, but gamely he held the roses in her direction. "I wanted to give you these."

She didn't shift her briefcase or her purse, but held onto both, making it clear that she didn't intend to accept the flowers. "Harry, we've been through this."

His rusty eyebrows dipped with apprehension. Taking her elbow, he prodded her off the sidewalk to a more private area among half a dozen dogwood trees. "Em, you can't be this unfeeling," he insisted anxiously. "Haven't I said I'm sorry? Can't you forgive me for one little mistake?"

One little mistake? She pulled from his hold, trying to keep her expression bland. After all, her students were milling around, waiting until the very last second before they had to enter their classrooms. She didn't want to make a scene. "Harry, I've already told you I forgive you. I'm even sorry this thing between you and Elsa didn't work out. But I'm not taking you back."

He sucked in a breath, looking like a scolded puppy. She'd never noticed how really ordinary Harry was. She'd always thought him rather attractive, but for some reason his tall, slender frame seemed frail and drab now. And his russet hair appeared thin and lifeless—rather like a plate of overripe grated carrots. Not even a vegetable she liked. She swallowed hard, hoping every man she met didn't have the same dreadful fate—being compared to one particular self-centered playboy.

"Em," Harry interrupted her dour train of thought. "I know I've told you this before, but it's just that you're so—so different from last May. You're more independent, you have such strength, and—oh, I don't know. You're so arousing, I guess is the word."

A blush of embarrassment crept up her face. "Harry, a smart woman doesn't get left at the church without learning a few things that will keep it from happening again."

"It won't happen again, honey," he said, his tone pleading.

She chuckled, but the sound was more tart than agreeable. "At least you're right about that." She eyed him levelly, deciding he needed to hear something straight out. "Look, Harry. I'm not the obliging, naive woman you ran out on. I was humiliated by what happened. I hated myself for being such a failure, and I wanted to change. So I went away and I met—I *learned* things about myself. And the first thing I learned was, though you weren't to blame for your feelings, you're a shallow jerk." His flinch didn't even faze her. "The second thing I learned was that, though I tried to shift the blame to you and my father for my failures, I realized I couldn't. I'm responsible for myself. Maybe Dad's overbearing personality was partly to blame, but Elsa had the same father, and she left." Shrugging, she turned away. "I stayed, trying to please. I just didn't have the same wanderlust in my soul. So my staying really had little to do with Daddy browbeating me into submission. I *liked* being a teacher. The only thing I'd like more is to raise my own children." When he started to speak, she frowned him down. "Don't even say it, Harry. They won't be *your* children."

His face fell, and he looked so tragic Emily had to clear her throat to keep her voice even. "I know now I'm a good teacher. And, thanks to your desertion, I've found out what's worthy and right about who I am, and I discovered I'm proud of that."

"But, Em—"

"So, Harry," she interrupted. "What you see now is the same Emily I've always been. I've just been made aware of my self-worth." It was ironic that a shallow, cold-blooded playboy had taught her the most significant lesson in her life, but it was true. With a huge exhale, she finished, "I'm happy with *me*, Harry."

"You should be. It shines out of you like a candle," he mumbled plaintively.

She smiled at him, feeling pity. He was suffering so, poor man. But she couldn't help him. She had troubles in that area of her own. "Thank you, Harry. I hope we can be friends."

She watched his Adam's apple bob with dismay. "Is that all we can be, Em? Are you sure?"

She nodded. "That's all. Please accept this as my final word." Glancing at her wristwatch, she murmured, "I have to go." Without the heart to look into his sad brown eyes, she dashed up the steps into the building. No one knew better than she how hard it was to get on with your life after your heart had been broken. But she had a feeling Harry finally understood it was time for him to move on. She wished him luck.

She'd lied to him, of course—at least about one thing. She was far from happy. She knew she was a stronger person for meeting Lyon, but she wasn't really living. She was surviving, existing, trying to cope with an impossible love. But she was far from happy. Now that Meg was pregnant and bubbling over with impending motherhood, Emily hoped she could take on the cheerful mantle of doting godmother and force Lyon Gallant to the back of her heart and soul.

Noise abounded in the hallway as students gathered in clusters, looking at schedules and squealing excitedly when they discovered they had classes together or groaning and grousing when they didn't.

She was running late and picked up her pace. She'd wanted to have several instructions copied on the blackboard before the first bell. Swinging around the corner into her room, she stopped dead, her briefcase thudding to the scarred wood. A man, so tall, broad-shouldered and gorgeous that he couldn't be mistaken for a student, lounged against her desk. His profile was contemplative.

At the crash of her briefcase, he turned toward her. Then he grinned. At the stunning show of teeth, her purse followed her briefcase to the floor, scattering compact, lipstick and other clattery things about her feet.

Dark eyes glittered with soft amusement. "Is this dropping of accessories a traditional Iowa ceremony for the first day of school?"

She swallowed, not believing her eyes and ears. He pushed away from the desk and came toward her, his gait as graceful and seductive as she remembered. When he reached her, she timidly leaned against the doorjamb with no idea how to react.

He didn't touch her, but hunkered down, replacing her things in her purse. He stood and tucked her bag under one arm and carried it along with her briefcase to the desk. She didn't move.

When he turned back, the amusement in his gaze was gone. "Emily? What does that look mean?"

She shook her head, unable to find her voice, still trying to comprehend what was happening.

He strode to her, taking her limp hands in his big, warm ones. When his fingers touched hers, desire rushed at her like a great wave, but she fought the feeling.

"Let me try this again." He tugged her into the room, his expression gentle. "I'm new here. Is this Psychology 101?"

"Lyon?" she managed in a squeak. "What—what..." She didn't dare ask, didn't dare hope.

He lifted her fingers to his lips, kissing them, sending ripples of pleasure through her. She went weak, and her breathing grew labored. She couldn't draw away from the caress of his lips, though she knew it would be the wise move.

"Emily, you were right about your analysis the last night on the island." Lowering her hand but continuing to hold it, he smiled at

her with his lips and his eyes. "I did feel
hollow, empty, but I never knew why, until a
lovely, shy woman tripped over me one
morning, asking for something she never
lacked."

She heard a giggle, and her gaze flitted
around. Students were arriving, taking seats,
gawking, but she couldn't react. Her glance
lifted on its own to Lyon's face again. Oh,
those eyes. They held a startling sweetness,
and glimmered, almost as though they were
damp with tears.

He took her face between strong, gentle
hands. "I never analyzed it, but building that
cabin made me feel at peace—somehow more
whole. With everything I had, I didn't need
that cabin, yet somewhere deep inside, I did.
I needed what building it gave me." His gaze
moved over her face, and she could tell he was
trying to decipher her expression. She felt for
him, for she had no idea what she was feeling
herself. She was so numb and confused.

Bending toward her, he kissed the corners
of her mouth. "With you in my arms that day
on the beach, I got a glimpse of that same
peace and wholeness. But I fought what I felt
for you. I didn't need some quaintly con-

servative woman in my life. I had any beautiful toy I wanted, any time I wanted. My feelings for you made no sense, the way building that cabin made no sense."

She heard a sigh and wasn't sure if it had issued from her own throat or from some female student. But she didn't care. She was staring into the eyes of a man who was telling her something extraordinary. Unbelievable. Right out of her fondest dreams. *Meaning it.*

She opened her lips to speak, but no sound came.

At her continued silence, he shook his head, looking uncertain and aggravated with himself. "Dammit, I've been rambling on and left off the most important part." His scent, his essence tantalized her nostrils as he smiled at her. "I love you, Emily," he whispered, and suddenly it was all there in his eyes, so profound, so real. "Will you marry me?"

There were squeals, whoops and guttural laughter. Her face went crimson. They had quite an enthralled audience, it seemed. Lyon spared the youngsters a rankled glance, then returned his gaze to her. "Please, say something."

The hint of anguish in his voice shook her out of her stupor. "You—you love me?" she asked so quietly she hardly heard the query herself.

He chuckled wryly. "I've taken up solitary jogging since you left. Do you need any more proof than that?"

Emily felt a new fullness in her heart with his gentle teasing, and an incomparable gladness engulfed her. "Oh, Lyon," she breathed. "I've loved you for so long..."

His expression eased, growing so utterly loving it brought tears of joy to her eyes. "That's what I needed to hear, sweetheart," he murmured, lifting her into his arms.

Delirious, she hugged his neck. Taking that as an invitation to kiss her, he repeated his eternal vow against her lips, amid giggles and applause.

His kiss was hot and restless for deeper fulfillment, and she reveled in the depth of his desire. A piercing sweetness overpowered her. Oh, how she loved this man, with a love as strong as—no, stronger than—her need to breathe.

Once she realized he'd taken her out of her classroom and was leaving the school with her, she protested weakly, "My class!"

"I've arranged for a substitute." His eyes shone with devotion and promise. "For the next few years, sweetheart, you'll be too busy having our babies to worry about teaching."

Unable to believe her good fortune, she snuggled in his arms, so full of contentment she was afraid she would burst. "You think of everything, don't you?"

"Uh-huh." His tone was deep and erotic. She had a feeling his thoughts were very definitely on teaching her lesson number four.

Lesson four!

As she kissed him, the staggering truth finally began to sink in. *She* was the woman who had won the unattainable Lyon Gallant. And no one in his right mind could call her an expert in the field of seduction! With this man loving her, she would never feel like a failure again. *Lyon, darling,* she pledged silently, *just wait until I've had a little practice! You'll be a very happy husband!*

Her giggle drew his puzzled gaze, but she only kissed him warmly, sighing. "I hope the cabin is finished. I'd like to spend our honeymoon there."

"It is." He nibbled at her earlobe. "When I wasn't jogging, I did a hell of a lot of hammering."

Their laughter mingled as they began their lives together. At last, the shy teacher found her true love, and the worldly millionaire discovered what all his wealth and power could never give him.

Real happiness.